A Town Called Innocence

Will Bennett is down on his luck with a vengeance. Falsely convicted of murder and sentenced to hang, it seems as though the end of his young life is in sight. But he has an astounding change of fortune, and a strange circumstance of fate frees him to track down the man who was really responsible for the murder of Amelia Dyson, of which he was wrongly accused.

His journey takes him to the Texas town of Sherman. Here, he learns the truth about the plot which nearly sent him to the gallows. Bennett's journey from the town called Innocence to the final showdown with the man who framed him for murder ends in a bloody shootout, from which only one man will emerge alive.

A Town Called Innocence

Simon Webb

A Black Horse Western

ROBERT HALE · LONDON

ISBN 978-0-7198-1689-5

Robert Hale Limited
Clerkenwell House
Clerkenwell Green
London EC1R 0HT

www.halebooks.com

Typeset by
Derek Doyle & Associates, Shaw Heath
Printed and bound in Great Britain by
CPI Antony Rowe, Chippenham and Eastbourne

CHAPTER 1

The gaily painted red Concorde rattled across the bleak, dusty landscape. There were only four passengers within the stage; two men and two women. One of the women was middle-aged and her companion so young that she had not yet begun to put up her hair. From the look of them, it seemed likely that they were mother and daughter. The two men sitting opposite presented a much greater contrast. The elder of these two was a stern-looking individual; clad in sober, clerical black, but displaying a gleaming silver star upon the lapel of his jacket. The young man sitting next to him wore a defeated, hangdog expression, as though he had practically given up on life. His right wrist was linked to that of the man at his side by bright, steel handcuffs.

Although the two men had been on the coach since it left Sherman, some hours ago, the women had only got on at a little way-halt, a few minutes earlier. They had since then spoken quietly to each

5

other, but not exchanged a single word with the other passengers. Perhaps it was the grim aspect of the older of the two men, with his iron-grey moustache and cold eyes, or perhaps it was the glimpse of the length of chain which indicated that here was a prisoner with his escort. For whatever reason, the older woman had, after one brief glance, ignored the men entirely, although her young companion darted curious looks at the two of them from time to time.

At length, the man sporting the star spoke. He said, 'I wasn't eavesdropping, ma'am, but I couldn't help but hear what you said to the driver when you boarded. You're affeared on account of we're cutting through the Indian Nations. Is that right?'

'Why, yes,' said the woman, plainly pleased that somebody else had broken the ice and begun a conversation. 'To speak plainly, I am.'

'Well then, you've no occasion to be so. We'll lose two days off the journey to Kansas by taking this short cut and it's worth it. The Chickasaw are at peace and so are the other four civilized tribes. You'll see, it's all as safe as safe can be. It's a valuable short cut, nothing more.'

The woman looked relieved to receive such reassurance, until the surly-looking younger man, who hadn't yet said a word, remarked quietly, 'They say short cuts make for long delays. Or, as my grandpappy had it, long cut draws sweat; short cut draws blood.'

The man next to him said in a low, savage voice,

'Hush your mouth, you fool. You'll be scaring the ladies directly. What ails you?'

The other shrugged and limited himself to observing, 'There's other hazards, 'sides Indians.'

This brief conversation had evidently reawakened the woman's apprehensions, because she said, 'What does your friend mean by other hazards, Sheriff?'

'Marshal, if you please ma'am. Marshal Ebenezer Curtis at your service. And I'm bound to remark as this fellow is no friend of mine. I'm a taking Mr Bennett here to the federal penitentiary, ain't that right, Mr Bennett?'

The man so addressed said nothing and merely gazed moodily from the window. There was an uncomfortable silence, broken this time by the girl, who asked, 'Are you going all the way to Topeka, sir?'

'I am, God willing,' replied Marshal Curtis piously. 'You have the advantage of me, though, Miss. I don't mind that I caught your name.'

The older woman said, 'I'm sorry, Marshal, the fault is entirely mine. I am Mrs Marie Lowry and this here is my daughter Arabella.'

'Though folks generally call me Bella,' interposed the girl.

'My daughter's been at school in Baton Rouge and now my husband and I feel it's time that she began to enter polite society.'

'I'm sure she'll grace society with her presence,' said the marshal gallantly.

This was the sort of pointless talk that Will Bennett

never had been able to abide. He closed his eyes and allowed the swaying motion of the stagecoach to lull him slowly into a state poised between wakefulness and slumber. In this drowsy condition, he let his mind wander back to the events which had led him to such a pass. Like a man who has just lost a game of poker with ruinously high stakes, Bennett tried to work out where things had gone wrong and if he could have played the cards he'd been dealt more skillfully and not ended up in this present fix.

When the War Between the States had drawn to its bitter and inevitable close three years earlier, Bennett had been a private soldier in the army of the Confederacy. Like many of the young men who had spent five years fighting in various parts of the country, Will Bennett had found it difficult, indeed impossible, to settle down to a routine and humdrum life after the signing of the surrender at Appomattox Courthouse. Instead, he continued the nomadic way of life for which he had acquired a taste during the war; drifting from town to town, state to state; never settling long in any one place. At different times in the course of the last three years, he had worked as cowboy, barkeep, street sweeper, labourer and even deputy sheriff. His wandering had taken him as far north as Pennsylvania and all the way south to Louisiana.

In early May, he had fetched up in the little town of Innocence, not far north of Dallas, and soon afterwards Will Bennett began to think that he had really fallen on his feet. He was ambling along the road leading into Innocence, just another travel-stained saddletramp, when he had been hailed from a nearby field. A man had called, 'Hey, pilgrim! Come over here and slake your thirst. You surely look like you and that horse of your'n could do with a rest.'

This was his first meeting with Mick Dyson, a farmer whose fields Bennett had happened to be riding by. Learning that the other man was a little down on his luck, Dyson had offered him the chance to stay in his barn for a spell and eat with him and his wife; all in exchange for a little work around the farm. It looked to Will Bennett like the answer to his prayers. Mr and Mrs Dyson were an agreeable couple and they had both made him welcome. They struck Bennett as warm and friendly folks. That first meal with them, he had confided about the problem from which he had suffered since the Battle of Atlanta. He had been struck a glancing blow on the head by a minie ball; not severe enough to shatter his skull, but of sufficient power to effect a mischief in his brain. Since that day, he had been prey to excruciating head pains, which took him at irregular intervals. Worse than that, following these attacks, he was prone to memory loss, of such a nature that it was not uncommon for him to lose all recollection of lengths of time varying between fifteen minutes and half a day. In spite of this, both the Dysons were eager for him to stay for a spell.

For better than a se'night, all went well. Then, on

the morning of Tuesday 19 May, disaster fell. Mick Dyson had to go to Dallas for the day and did not expect to be back until long after nightfall. He told Will what needed doing, kissed his wife goodbye and trotted off south to the big city. That evening, Bennett ate with Mrs Dyson as usual and then retired to the hayloft. He was not feeling at his best and prayed that he was not about to be afflicted with his old disorder. His head ached and there were the warning, shimmery haloes around objects, which suggested to him that he was about have one of his 'turns'. He thought, under the circumstances, that the best thing would be to get his head down and try to sleep as soon as possible.

In his pocket, Will Bennett had a page of a newspaper which he had got hold of after the trial in Dallas. He had read this through so many times that he knew it almost by heart. It was from the Friday, 12 June 1868 edition of the *Dallas County Advertiser; Incorporating the Fort Worth Agricultural Intelligencer and Gazette* and it read as follows:

Readers of this newspaper living not only in our own fair city, but also in and around the town of Innocence, will have been shocked and distressed some weeks ago to learn of the murder of Mrs AMELIA DYSON, wife of local farmer MICHAEL DYSON. It will be recollected from reports at the time that Mr DYSON had, as an act of Christian charity, given shelter and sustenance to a drifter by the name of WILLIAM BENNETT.

The aforementioned BENNETT had been granted licence to sleep in the hayloft of a barn and allowed to partake of meals with Mr and Mrs DYSON, in exchange for working around the farm.

BENNETT's ingratitude for this kind treatment, as has now been proved in a court of law, surpassed all reason. On the 19 ultimo, Mr DYSON came to Dallas on business of an agricultural nature. Returning late that night to his home near Innocence, he encountered a scene of unparalleled horror. Entering the kitchen of his farmhouse, he found his wife lying dead. She had been stabbed repeatedly and with the utmost ferocity. Being a family newspaper, common decency forbids us to harrow readers with the precise details; suffice it to say that the poor woman had also been subjected to an outrageous violation of the most depraved character.

Checking on BENNETT, Mr DYSON found his hired man asleep in the barn, smelling strongly of whiskey and with his hands and clothes splashed liberally with blood. The man could give no account of himself and he was soon afterwards delivered up to the local sheriff, Mr PATRICK O'KEEFE. So strong was feeling running against the accused man, that Sheriff

O'KEEFE feared that an attempt might be made to storm his office in Innocence and invite BENNETT to a 'Necktie Party'. He consequently arranged for his prisoner to be transferred to Dallas for trial. So conclusive was the evidence against BENNETT that the jury did not even take the trouble to retire in order to consider their verdict, announcing at the end of the trial that they had heard enough and wished to bring the accused man in guilty at once.

Judge CROWTHER passed sentence of death and WILLIAM BENNETT is scheduled to hang publicly some time next week.

Bennett was roused from his reverie by the high, clear voice of Arabella Lowry, saying, 'Oh look, Mama, those men are racing us. What a lark!'

Her mother looked out of the window and then sat back, having turned a little pale. Marshal Curtis said, 'Nothing wrong, I hope, ma'am?'

'Marshal, might I trouble you to take a peep from the window on this side and give me your opinion?'

'Why surely, Mrs Lowry.'

One look was enough to spur Curtis into action. He turned to Bennett and said urgently, 'I have to speak to the fellow up atop who's riding shotgun. Stand up, so's I can lean out of the window and have some conversation with him.'

'Like I said,' remarked Bennett quietly, as he got

to his feet, 'there's other hazards in these parts, 'side Indians.'

The marshal gave him a sharp look, saying, 'You know aught of this? Those boys wouldn't be friends o' yours, I suppose?'

'Don't know that I have any friends,' said Bennett. 'Whatever's afoot is no affair of mine.'

The wind whistling past the stage obscured the marshal's words as he leaned out the window and spoke to the driver and his partner. Neither Bennett nor either of the women caught a single word. However, when he sat down again, Marshal Curtis caused the greatest alarm to Mrs Lowry by taking his pistol from its holster and checking that it was loaded and the cylinder spinning smoothly. 'Lord a mercy,' she said, 'What's to do?'

'I won't deceive you, ma'am. I don't care over-much for the look of those three men keeping pace with us there. I hope it doesn't signify, but there's no harm in being prepared.'

For answer, Mrs Lowry put her arm around her daughter and drew her closer. Arabella said, 'Who are those men? I don't understand.'

Bennett said casually, 'I dare say Curtis here thinks as those boys are road agents. Like the old time high-waymen in England, you know.'

'Oh, how thrilling!' said the girl. 'Are they going to hold us up?'

'Hush up, child,' said her mother, 'and don't talk to that man. He's a prisoner of the marshal here and the Good Lord alone knows what he's done.'

There was the crack of a rifle and then an answering boom from much closer at hand. Bennett guessed that one of the riders had fired at the driver and that the other fellow up there had then let fly with a scattergun. Then there were two more shots. Marshal Curtis had his gun in his hand and was peering from the windows, trying to mark a target.

'You're wasting your time,' Bennett told him. 'They know that dodge. Those fellows'll be riding right behind us now, so's none of the passengers can take pot shots at 'em.' He addressed the woman and her daughter. 'You'd do well to get down on the floor, the two of you. It'll lessen the risk of catching a stray ball.' They took his advice, the woman huddling over her daughter, so that if any bullet did enter the coach, it would strike her first.

The end of the pursuit came with shocking swiftness. Because of the driver's reluctance to bring the Concorde to a halt, the men behind them fired at the horses, killing one. The dead weight was too much for the remaining three animals and the coach began to slow. Even so, the driver and fellow riding shotgun showed that they were determined to keep going, with the natural result that they too were shot. The driver toppled from his seat and fell to the ground. With the reins slack, the three horses continued for a time until, losing all patience, the three riders fired another half dozen shots and killed first

14

one and then another of the beasts.

Marshal Curtis had still not been able to get a good shot at the attackers. He kept trying to dodge from one side of the coach to the other, looking to the rear in hope of a clear field of fire. An irksome circumstance for both the marshal and his prisoner was that they needed to cooperate with perfect timing for Curtis to have any chance of success. Since Will Bennett was indifferent to the peril in which they found themselves, already facing the prospect of being hanged, he could not summon up much enthusiasm for jumping around the interior of the coach, solely to make life easier for Curtis.

When the stagecoach finally ground to a halt, there was, for a moment, complete silence. Then the passengers heard the drumming of hoofs as the men who had been chasing them drew near. Bennett said to the marshal, 'Throw down your weapon and let them see that we are unarmed. They might leave us be and content themselves with what's in that box stowed at the back there.'

'Yes, you'd like that, wouldn't you?' asked Marshal Curtis with a sneer. 'There's not a chance. I'll brace those scallywags by my own self.' He was as good as his word, because as the first rider came into view, the marshal leaned out and shot him. It was the only shot he managed to get off, because one of the other men, coming up from behind, had a perfect target in the back of Curtis's head. He drew down on the marshal, fired and blew half the man's brains out.

Bennett muttered to himself with quiet satisfaction, 'Just as I thought would happen.'

The man Curtis had shot was more angry than anything about the wound he had received. It was not a serious one; amounting only to a long graze on his upper arm, which had scarcely broken the skin. His pride was injured more badly than his flesh, because he began to shout, 'I'll kill the bastard who did this, you hear what I say?'

Will Bennett called to the three men, all of whom had neckerchiefs pulled up over the lower half of their faces, like they might be acting the part of bandits in a play, 'There's two frightened women in here and me. I'm unarmed. The man who shot you's dead.'

'That bein' so,' shouted one of the riders, 'you all three of you best come out with your hands held high. I tell you now, it won't take much for us to kill the whole boilin' of you.'

'Get up and leave the coach,' said Bennett to Mrs Lowry and her daughter. 'Quickly now; they mean just what they say. Our lives are hangin' by a thread here.'

Fearfully, mother and daughter got to their feet and climbed down to the ground. Will Bennett stayed where he was. The man who had spoken before said, 'You too, fellow. I'm telling you, my patience is all wore away.'

'It'll take me some time to get out,' called back Bennett, 'on account of I'm chained up to the man

16

as was shootin' at you boys.'

'The hell you are! What are you, convict or something of the sort?'

'That's right. Don't be getting twitchy now, 'cause it's no easy thing to drag a man's corpse about.'

It was, as Bennett had intimated to the other man, a tricky proceeding to manhandle a dead body when you are attached to the same by a short steel chain. Nevertheless, he eventually managed it and stood blinking in the sunlight with Marshal Curtis lying dead, his arm raised up by the handcuff which linked it to Bennett's own wrist. The three men who had ambushed the stage found the sight highly diverting. 'Hoo, boy,' said one of them, 'what you goin' to do when that body starts rotting? You gonna be draggin' a skeleton round with you.'

'Recollect that there's a lady present and a young girl too,' said Bennett quietly. 'Such talk ain't fittin'.'

'Well,' said another of the men, 'we best think on what to do next. I never seed a situation such as this in the whole course of my life.'

'Before you go further,' said Bennett, 'you might assure these two that you mean 'em no harm and that they can rest easy.'

'Oh, as to that, we only want what this here stage was transportin' 'cross the territories. Got no interest in womenfolk or anything else. You needn't fret none, ma'am. Nor you neither, miss.'

Bennett nodded. He wasn't overfond of bushwhackers and road agents, but these three didn't appear to him to be especially bad examples of the breed. He said, 'Well then, I guess we'll just wait on your pleasure.'

CHAPTER 2

The three men who had waylaid the stage dismounted and went round to the back of the vehicle. The suitcases belonging to Mrs Lowry were secured there under a 'paulin and she exhibited some anxiety when she saw that the men were, as she thought, meddling with her luggage. She looked as though she might be on the verge of expostulating with them, until Bennett said softly, so that the road agents couldn't hear, 'Ma'am, were I you, I'd say nothing to aggravate those fellows. We're not out of the woods yet, not by a long sight.'

It appeared that the men had not the least interest in Mrs Lowry's cases, being concerned only with a small, wooden crate which had been concealed beneath the Lowrys' luggage. This they hoisted out and then forced open with a length of metal. Bennett was curious to know what was in the box, which had, he guessed, been the whole object of the raid on the stage. Inside, wrapped in little screws of tissue paper were what looked to Bennett to be the stock of a not very prosperous jeweller's shop. There were silver watch chains, gold earbobs, rings and other little gewgaws. He was no expert, but it hardly seemed like a treasure trove. 'Was that worth the lives of three men?' he asked, wonderingly.

'Heard that a fellow in Sherman was shuttin' up shop and moving his business across to Kansas,' said the man who had jemmied open the wooden box. 'Still, you're right. I might o' expected somewhat more than this haul.'

As the man spoke, he and his two companions were dividing up the contents of the box between them; unwrapping the jewellery and transferring it to their saddle-bags. Will Bennett and the two Lowrys stood by watching, not knowing yet how matters would develop with regard to themselves. They soon found out. Having emptied the crate of everything it had contained, the three robbers held a brief, whispered consultation and one of them then said, 'Well, we must be gettin' on. We'll bid you folks a very good day and hope that you ain't stranded out here for too long.' Then he mounted up, as did the other two. Bennett stepped forward, before being pulled up short by the chain on his wrist, which kept him securely anchored to the marshal's corpse.

'You'd leave these ladies out here in the wilderness, alone?' said Will Bennett angrily. 'I reckon I can take care of my own self, but these two? What sort of men are you?'

'You watch your mouth, mister,' said the man who had, throughout the whole affair, acted as the spokesman for the gang. 'We're leavin' 'em their lives and honour intact, which is more than some fellows in our line o' work would do. Be thankful on it.' Then he spurred on his horse and a second later, all three of the men were galloping away.

Mrs Lowry and her daughter looked quite perplexed and watched Bennett closely, as though he were about to perform some miracle, perhaps bringing the horses and driver back to life so that they could complete their journey across the territories. Well, one thing was for certain sure: he would be able to do nothing at all as long as he was inextricably linked to a dead man. Bennett said to the girl, 'I need your help, miss.' Seeing the look of alarm on her mother's face, he continued hurriedly, 'It's nothing untoward. I want you to scoot over to the stage and look for a box holding some tools. There'd be a hammer, saw and suchlike in it.' Seeing the blank look on the girl's face, he explained, 'Sometimes axles break, repairs needs must be carried out. There's sure to be a wood saw somewhere about. I want you to fetch it for me, if you please.'

All things considered, both mother and daughter were bearing up pretty well, thought Bennett. After all, they had seen three men slain in close proximity to them, been jumped by bushwhackers and were now stranded in the middle of nowhere with a man who was being taken under close escort to the federal penitentiary. Neither of them showed any signs of having a fit of the hysterics and both seemed willing to follow his advice.

Arabella Lowry poked about gingerly in the luggage compartment of the stagecoach without finding anything that might have been a toolbox. Then she looked inside and was about to climb up on to the driver's seat when she noticed for the first time that another corpse lay sprawled there; its limbs contorted like a marionette whose strings had been cut. 'Oh,' she cried in disgust, 'what shall I do now?'

'You wish to get to safety,' Bennett told her, 'you'll carry on huntin' for that saw I need.'

The girl's face wrinkled, like she had a bad smell in her nostrils, but she followed his advice and peered under the driver's seat. Then she gave a little cry of triumph and pulled out a rusty old wood saw, which had been lying next to a few other bits and pieces. 'Shall I bring it to you?' she called down to Bennett.

'It'd be a sight easier than me hauling the late Marshal Curtis up there to fetch it,' said Bennett sourly. While the girl had been looking for the saw, Bennett had been methodically searching the marshal's pockets, without success, which proceeding had been watched disapprovingly by Mrs Lowry. He didn't feel it necessary to tell her that he was hunting for the key to the handcuffs.

Once he had the saw in his hand, Bennett drew

the blade tentatively across the steel links of the handcuffs. It proved just as useless and ineffectual as he had thought would be the case. He said to Mrs Lowry, 'Ma'am, I'd be greatly obliged if you could take your daughter round to the other side of the stage for a few minutes.'

'Round the other side of the stagecoach?' asked the woman in bewilderment. 'Whatever for?'

'I'll explain later. Please, it will only be for five minutes or so, no longer.'

The older woman stared at him oddly, as though he had taken leave of his senses, but finally consented to do as he asked. 'Come along, Bella,' she said, 'I'm hoping that Mr Bennett here has some sort of plan or the Lord knows what will become of us.'

Once he was sure that the two of them were out of sight and sound, Bennett squatted down on the ground and stretched out Curtis's arm on the ground. Then he began sawing firmly at the dead man's wrist. It was a messy business and the blunt, rusty blade made heavy weather of the bone, but in less than five minutes he had succeeded in severing the hand from the body and was free of the corpse. The handcuffs were slippery with blood, but that couldn't be helped. He walked round to where the two women were waiting. 'Oh, how clever!' exclaimed Bella Lowry, 'you're free. However did you. . . .' Her voice tailed off as she caught sight of the congealed blood which was smeared around the handcuff hanging from his wrist. She clapped her hands to her mouth in shock.

Bennett was annoyed with himself for presenting the girl with such a disagreeable sight and covered his feelings by remarking gruffly, 'Needs must when the Devil drives.'

Now that he was free, Bennett went over the vehicle carefully, to see what resources were to be found. They were slender enough. There was a little food, a keg of drinking water, along with a couple of canteens and also the Lowrys' luggage. The only other items which would come in handy were Marshal Curtis's pistol, the scattergun, which had been used by the fellow riding shotgun and two flasks of powder. Curtis's pockets had also yielded up a box of caps and a few balls and wads of lint.

For the next quarter hour, Bennett ignored the women and occupied himself with cleaning and loading both firearms. Mrs Lowry and her daughter stood a little way off, conferring quietly together. When he'd finished loading the guns, Will Bennett went over to the water cask and filled the two canteens. Then he stopped for a moment and reasoned out his next course of action.

For the first time since Michael Dyson had roused him at gunpoint and delivered him into the custody of the sheriff of Innocence, Will Bennett was a free man. He was fit, healthy and armed. Doubtless, it would now be possible for him to make his way out of the Indian Nations and emerge in Arkansas, say; quite unknown and in no worse a case than he was

24

before he had first arrived in Innocence. It was an alluring prospect, but he did not really consider it for a moment, because such a course of action would have been contingent upon abandoning a woman and her young daughter alone in the wild and giving no further thought about their welfare. Even as he idly turned over the notion of escaping to Arkansas alone and unencumbered, Bennett knew that it was the merest fantasy and that he couldn't do it. He'd never sleep easy again in his life if he undertook such a callous and dishonourable action.

Having filled up the canteens, Bennett went over to where the mother and daughter stood, presumably awaiting his instructions. He said to the girl, 'Tell me, miss, what age have you?'

'I'll be seventeen next month.'

He turned to the mother and said, 'And you thought it would be a right smart idea to travel with a girl of that age across the Indian Nations, did you, ma'am?'

'They told us it was the quicker route," said Mrs Lowry defensively. 'Even the marshal thought it was safe.'

'The marshal, God rest his soul, was a damned fool.' As soon as the word was out, Bennett was sorry. Mrs Lowry looked scandalized. He said to the girl, 'I do beg your pardon, miss. It just slipped out.'

To his surprise and also that of her mother, Arabella Lowry said, 'You needn't mind me. I heard worse than that in Baton Rouge. And please don't call me "miss". It makes me feel positively ancient. Everybody calls me Bella.'

Despite this permission, the greatest liberty that Bennett would permit himself was to address her in the future as 'Miss Bella'. 'And now,' he said, 'we got to work out the best course of action. By my calculation, we've come something like fifty miles since the pair o' you boarded this here stage. Now I don't believe for a moment that you two could walk fifty miles back again. I'm accustomed to such things and it would take even me a two day march and I don't see that you two would make it at all. All else apart, those fancy shoes would fall to pieces after the first couple o' miles.'

'What do you propose then, Mr Bennett?' asked Mrs Lowry sharply. 'That we just sit down here and wait to die?'

He smiled at her and said, 'You got pepper, ma'am. No, I don't think as we should give up. If we can't go back, then we must go forward. This stage must have been expecting to change horses before much longer and so I say we should carry on in the direction as we was travelling. But it ain't as easy as that.'

'How so?'

'You might not know it,' said Bennett, trying to put the case as delicately as he could and not shock the sensibilities of the women, 'but we were lucky with those fellows as ambushed us.'

'Lucky!' said Mrs Lowry. 'God preserve us from

such good fortune in the future. What can you mean by it, sir?'

'I'm saying as there are those who might have taken advantage of the situation, with two women who lacked a male protector. Those boys only wanted their box o' baubles and gave no thought to such a thing.'

It was plain that this had not before occurred to Mrs Lowry, because she went a little pale; less, thought Bennett shrewdly, for the peril to herself, but most likely thinking about what might have befallen her child. She limited herself to observing, 'You're a blunt speaker, sir.'

'I've no time to be otherwise. We need to get off the road and out of sight and that right quick.'

'I thought you wanted us to make our way onwards?'

'Yes, but not on the open road. I'd feel easier in my mind if we could advance a little circuitous, like. There's not only the chance of running into road agents; there's also Indians to think of.'

'I understood it to be the case that we were at peace with the Chickasaw. That, at least, was what I apprehended from the marshal.'

'I don't like to speak ill of the dead,' said Bennett, 'which is not a gracious thing to do, but Curtis didn't know . . . what he was talkin' 'bout. I dare say that they'd not interfere with a coach, for fear of bringing the army down on them. But travellers like us, wandering in their lands is something else again. I tell you straight: we need to be on our guard.'

'Very well, my daughter and I seem to be in your hands, Mr Bennett. What do you say we ought to do?'

'First off is where you should drink as much of the water from that there keg as you can. We only have these two small canteens to carry it in and you'll find you soon dry out in this terrain. Then we must make for that little dip in the land, over yonder. It's a dried up water course. We should be able to make our way in the right direction, without being visible from the road.'

After they had all three of them drunk as much water as they could, Bennett buckled on the marshal's gunbelt and picked up the shotgun, which was fitted with a rudimentary sling. There was little food, but what there was he packed into a bag which one of those atop the stage had been carrying and then indicated that it was time to be moving off.

Mrs Lowry evinced a reluctance to leave the two corpses without making any provision for their interment. 'What will become of them?' she asked.

'Get ate up by wild animals, I dare say,' said Bennett and then immediately regretted speaking so plainly. He added, 'Doesn't scripture tell us as we should let the dead bury the dead? That about fits the present case, I should say.'

Neither of his companions was very athletic or used to walking long distances, from all that Bennett was able to collect. The girl was marginally more adept at walking on rough ground than her mother,

28

but that wasn't saying a great deal, as Mrs Lowry made very heavy weather of the whole business. Bennett began to wonder if they might not have been better just sitting by the stagecoach and waiting for somebody to come and rescue them. However, he had overheard a conversation between Curtis and the driver, when they started out from Sherman, which led him to suppose that there were only two coaches a week along this route. It would have been madness to sit there waiting for three or four days. No, he knew that he had done the right thing, but Lord, this promised to be a hard row to hoe and no mistake.

They stopped when they reached the little valley, which amounted really to no more than the dried up bed of a stream. Mrs Lowry said, when they had sat down for a brief rest, 'Would it be indelicate of me to inquire into the nature of the infraction which led to your being taken to the penitentiary, Mr Bennett? We're apt to be spending a deal of time in each other's company and I'd like to know how things stand.'

At first, the man said nothing and Mrs Lowry wondered if he had heard or was reluctant to answer such a straight question. At length, though, he replied slowly, 'Why, the truth is, ma'am, I was convicted in Dallas of an infamous crime. My trial had been transferred to Dallas from the little town where I had been first accused, because there was a fear that I might be lynched.'

'Lynched!' exclaimed the woman in horror. 'Lord a mercy, I never heard of such a thing. This ain't that far south. They have lynching in these parts?'

'They do,' Bennett told her, 'if the offence is specially dreadful and revoltin'. Not often, but it happens, odd times.'

'I'm almost afraid to press the point, but I suppose having come so far, it would be cowardly to hold back. What were you convicted of?'

Will Bennett looked the anxious mother in the eye and replied, 'I was found guilty of the rape and murder of a young woman, ma'am.'

'Saints preserve us,' she cried, 'you never were? Well, I guess you'll be telling us that it was all a terrible error and you were as innocent of the crime as a newborn babe?'

'That would be a comforting reflection for us both, I dare say,' said Bennett, 'but I won't deceive you, ma'am. I don't know if I was responsible for that terrible act or not. I surely hope that I wasn't, but I could not take oath and swear to it.' Mrs Lowry looked at him inquiringly and so he briefly outlined the medical condition brought on by being struck by the minie ball. Then he continued, 'Anyways, once I was found guilty and sentenced to hang, some slick lawyer came forward and offered to work on my case for nothing. He called it pro something, I don't rightly recall the exact expression.'

'Pro bono publico,' supplied Mrs Lowry, still eyeing him closely.

'That's it, for a bet. You know somewhat about the law ma'am?'

'Not me. My husband. Go on with your story.'

'There's little enough to tell. After I was sentenced to hang and this lawyer fellow wanted to take on my case, he filed some sort of legal document, I don't rightly mind what. It halted the execution, though, and was meant to give me a new trial. Only thing was, folk in Dallas was getting restless about all the delays and wanted to see me hang as soon as could be. The details of this crime as I was accused of being so bad, you understand. So in the end, the sheriff's office in Dallas asked if Marshal Curtis would take me up to the federal penitentiary in Topeka, so I could wait there while they fixed up this here new trial. They figured as folk in Topeka wouldn't be so worked up about me and the things I was supposed to've done.'

After he had finished this recitation, Mrs Lowry said, 'Well I declare, I don't rightly know what to say now and that's the fact of the matter. You say you can't warrant on the Bible that you didn't commit this crime, but you don't think you did it, is that right?'

'Not 'less I had some kind of brainstorm, ma'am. Like that blow on the head I told you of, as I suffered during the battle of Atlanta, 'less that scrambled up my head so badly that I'd do something clean against my nature. I can't say more.'

'Well I don't believe a word of it!' declared Bella Lowry firmly. 'And neither do you, Mama. I can tell by the look in your eyes. Why, you heard how Mr Bennett stood up to those three robbers and spoke out to them in order to protect us. It's absurd to think he'd ... well, take advantage of a helpless woman. It's not true.'

Will Bennett looked up shyly and saw the fierce look in the girl's eyes. He was oddly moved by such faith in him, who was next door to being a perfect stranger. 'Thank you, Miss Bella,' he said quietly. 'I don't know when I last was so cheered and encouraged by such an opinion.'

'Yes well,' said the girl's mother, 'fine words butter no parsnips, as they used to say when I was a child. You've proved a good friend to us so far, Mr Bennett, that I will allow. I think we must set aside your past for the time being and focus all our efforts upon the present moment.'

'I couldn't've have expressed the case better myself, ma'am. Unless I miss my guess, we've a long road ahead of us now and like you, I say we need to travel down that first, 'fore we start considering aught else.'

CHAPTER 3

They camped that night in a little cave which, at some time in the past, floodwater had carved from the side of the river course. At least, Mrs Lowry and her daughter slept in this space. Will Bennett, sensible of the impropriety of two ladies sharing sleeping accommodation with a man to whom they were not related, announced that he would be taking his rest at some little distance from them. 'I'm a light sleeper,' he told them. 'I want to make certain that I'm on hand to make sure that anything as might disturb your slumbers is discouraged from coming nigh to you.'

'What dangers do you talk of, Mr Bennett?' asked Bella, her eyes shining with excitement. 'You mean Indians?'

Looking at her as she spoke, it seemed to Bennett that the girl was not really taking this whole episode seriously; treating it rather as some schoolgirl escapade. Well, that was good. There was no point in her being frightened out of her wits. 'I don't think we need to worry overmuch 'bout Indians, Miss Bella,' he said gravely. 'I'm thinking more of wild animals, wolves and such. Don't worry. I'll be a setting up on yonder rock with this here scattergun and I'll be sure to keep them away from you ladies. You may rest easy.'

'Would it not be a good idea to light a fire?' asked Mrs Lowry. 'I understood that animals in the wild are terrified of flames.'

'That's one idea, ma'am,' answered Bennett tactfully. 'Fire and smoke might ward off fierce beasts all right, but men might be drawn to investigate. I'd feel more comfortable if we just slipped along through this territory without drawing any attention to ourselves.'

'Yes, I see what you mean. We are very much in your hands, Mr Bennett. Order things as you think best. Come, Bella. We shall sleep now and leave Mr Bennett to his lonely vigil. Goodnight, sir.'

As the two of them walked towards the little hollow, the girl turned back and shouted cheerfully, 'Goodnight, Mr Bennett. Thank you for all your help and assistance.'

'Goodnight Miss Bella,' he called back, 'I hope you have pleasant dreams this night.'

Sitting on a rock above the old stream-bed, with the shotgun cradled in his arms, Bennett thought over the day's events. There had surely been a turn-around in his fortunes since that stage left

Sherman. He might have wished that he could have skipped away, free as a bird following the robbery, but there; he wasn't such a dog as to leave two defenceless females out in the wild with nobody to look after them. Mrs Lowry was a little sharp, but treated him politely. As for that Arabella girl, well; she was a caution. Behaving like she was on a Sunday school picnic outing. There was an innocence about the girl which touched Bennett's heart. She was lively and had a little of her mother's sharpness in her, but the world had not yet taught her to mistrust those around her. Despite the unpromising circumstances in which she had made his acquaintance, chained to a federal marshal, Miss Bella was prepared to take him as she found him and had shown herself unwilling to believe ill of the erstwhile prisoner. Was that innocence or goodness? He could not tell.

The man perched on his rock slept fitfully during the night; never wholly asleep, but seldom fully awake either. Bennett was confident that he would jerk into wakefulness if either man or beast came close to him. The night passed quietly, though, and at dawn, he stood up and stretched. He wished to do as much walking as possible in the cool of the early morning.

As he walked down the slope to where the two women had slept, he encountered Arabella Lowry, who had also evidently just woken up.

'Good morning, sir. Isn't it a lovely day?'

Bennett looked around him and said, 'Fair to middling. Would you wake your mother for me and tell her we need to get moving as soon as possible?'

The girl did not go immediately, but came closer and said, 'It's good of you to keep from my mother just what a pickle we're in. I appreciate it. She's more nervous than she seems, you know.'

'I thought the boot was on the other foot,' said Bennett in surprise. 'Kind o' figured that it was she protecting you and stopping you being fearful.'

'Not really. She doesn't really believe that anything can harm her and her family. On account of my father being a judge, you see. We're too important for folk to trouble as a rule.'

'Your pa's a judge? That's a facer and no mistake. I wonder what he'd make o' a fellow like me being alone out here with his womenfolk?'

'He'd be very grateful that you were taking such good care of us,' said the girl firmly and went off to awaken her mother.

After they had eaten about half the rations that remained, Bennett said, 'I'm hoping that we'll come across a trading post or something of that nature, if we carry on in our present track. There're such scattered all over the Indian Nations. Or a mission; something of that kind.'

Just as Bennett had suspected, the shoes that Mrs Lowry and her daughter were wearing had almost completely fallen to pieces before they set off after breaking their fast in the dawn's early light. The brief walk the day before along the stream-bed had proved more than enough. What are we going to do now? thought Bennett to himself. They sure as hell can't walk across this landscape with nothing at all to protect their feet; they'll be cut to pieces. This particular conundrum was solved when he saw in the distance a glimpse of white, which gave him reason to hope that there was some kind of building, not too far ahead of them. What a mercy that is, he thought.

As they came closer to the building, it could be seen that it was a small house, adjoined to a low, single-storey structure. Next to it stood a tiny chapel, with a prominent cross planted upon the roof. All the buildings were coated with a dazzling wash of white paint; they could be seen from miles around, which was no doubt the purpose.

'Looks to me like this is the abode of some missioners,' said Bennett, 'which is by way of being what you might term a stroke of luck. How are your feet holding up?'

'I don't know how much longer my shoes will last,' said Bella Lowry mournfully. 'Just look at the state of them. I don't think they were meant for expeditions like this.'

'What about yours, ma'am?'

'Mine are in a similar case. I shall be glad to rest up. This isn't a way of life that suits me, Mr Bennett.'

Bennett laughed. Then, feeling that he might sound discourteous, he said, 'I guess it's what you're used to. I never yet had a pair o' shoes that weren't intended for rough travel. You two come from finer stock, I reckon.'

It took them an hour and a half to reach the cluster of buildings and long before they'd got there, Bennett knew that something was amiss. He couldn't say how he knew; he'd never troubled to analyze what he always thought of to himself as his cat's sense for danger, but he was quite certain in his own mind that something was wrong. There was in fact no great mystery about it. Subconsciously, Will Bennett had noted that no figures had appeared near the white-washed buildings for the hour or more that he had had them under his observation. No wisp of smoke trickling up to the sky, which might have hinted at a cooking fire, no sign of life at all, in fact. Then again, judging from the look of them, those buildings had only recently been painted. They were far from being ancient or ruinous.

Of course, all these external clues could have suggested nothing more sinister than those running the little mission station going off to tackle an outbreak of smallpox or something like that. But Bennett knew and he was not fixing to lead the two women at his side into danger of any description. When they were only a few hundred yards from the place, he said, 'Here's where you two take a seat, while I scout out the lie of the land.'

'Is something wrong?' asked Bella.

There didn't seem to be any purpose in dissembling and so he replied, 'Yes, I'd say there is. But I don't know precisely what and so you and your mother might rest here until I find out.'

'Are we in danger, Mr Bennett?' asked Mrs Lowry. 'If so, I'm sure I'd just as soon know about it.'

'Truly, ma'am, I couldn't say. Could be I'm off on a snipe hunt, but I'd still sooner the two of you were out of the way.' What Bennett didn't say was that he wanted the women at some distance, just on the off-chance that gunplay began. The last thing you wanted at such a time was to be fretting about where an innocent bystander might be hiding or, worse still, jump up in your line of fire. If he was to do any shooting, he preferred to have a free hand over where he threw the lead.

Before setting off towards the mission station, Bennett took two caps from the little tin box he had found on Marshal Curtis's body and slipped them over the nipples of the scattergun. Then he cocked both hammers and walked slowly forward.

If somebody was drawing down on him from a window or a concealed position behind one of the walls, then Bennett saw no sign of it. His eyes were that sharp, he was satisfied that nobody was preparing an ambush. Nevertheless, he held the scattergun at his hip, ready to let fly with both barrels at the least excuse. The door to the church was standing ajar and that seemed to be as good a spot as any to investigate. The interior of the tiny place of worship was cool and dark, with that rich smell of beeswax which Bennett always associated in some way with sanctity.

Most churches had that same aroma; the scent of lovingly polished benches. He sniffed appreciatively.

A thorough search of the chapel failed to uncover anybody hiding under the pews or behind the altar. Next was what proved to be a schoolroom, with rows of pine desks. Bennett shook his head in amazement, baffled as always at the determination of the missioners and the lengths to which they would go to save souls. The schoolroom too was deserted, which left only the house.

A smart rapping on the door brought nobody and so, aware that he might be entering somebody's home for the flimsiest of reasons, Bennett turned the handle and opened the door. He found them in the kitchen, lying dead on the tiled floor. A man and woman, both shot through the head. By the look of them, they had not been dead long. Bennett squatted down and examined the pool of blood on the floor. He touched it with his finger and found that the very centre was just the faintest bit sticky. This suggested that the blood had been shed no more than three or four hours earlier. Recent enough for the killers still to be around somewhere. He looked out back and noted the horse grazing.

When he rejoined Mrs Lowry and her daughter, Bennett chose his words with the utmost care, unwilling to expose them, even vicariously, to the horror which he had lately seen. 'There's no danger to be feared,' he said. 'We can all go there without being uneasy. The owners aren't there and I think we can fill up our canteens and so on. I saw a well. Maybe pick up some food.'

Mrs Lowry was sharper than Bennett had given her credit for. She said, 'What are you keeping from us, Mr Bennett? I'd like to know, for I have my daughter to think of.'

'Well then,' he replied, 'if you put it like that, then those I guess were the owners of that little mission station are lying dead in the kitchen. They been shot.'

'That's straight talking, at any rate,' said Mrs Lowry. 'What do you suggest we do?'

'Like I said, I think we should go there and see if we can pick up some food and water to see us on our way. Could be that there'll be stouter shoes or boots than those either of you are wearin' right now.'

Bella and her mother looked at Bennett with undisguised horror. 'What?' said Mrs Lowry in a disgusted tone of voice, like it was the most infamous proposal she had ever heard in her life. 'You mean loot a dead person's home? I never heard the like!'

Will Bennett said nothing for a few seconds, gazing thoughtfully out to the distant horizon. Then he turned and looked the older woman straight in the eyes. 'You was kind enough to compliment me on my straight talkin' just now. Leastways, I took it to be a compliment. Here's some more straight talking. You two ladies aren't going to get much further in those flimsy shoes o' your'n. If we don't speed up our pace a mort, you're like to die of thirst, hunger or I

41

don't know what. You need strong footwear and those dead folk have no use for any shoes they owned in life.'

Bella Lowry stared intently at Bennett and then turned to her mother, saying, 'He's right, Mama. You know he is. We can't carry on another pace in these things.' She lifted her foot to display the tattered remnants of a once fashionable pair of dainty shoes.

'Well, child, I dare say you're right. Mr Bennett, we are in your hands. I'm sorry if I spoke sharply.'

'It's nothing at all, ma'am. These ways take a little getting used is all.'

'These ways?' asked Mrs Lowry. 'You mean your own way of life?'

Bennett shrugged and said, 'Let's not waste any more time.'

He had taken care to close the door to the kitchen before leaving and when he took the two women to the mission station, Bennett suggested that they waited in the cool school-room, while he had a look round the house for some shoes. They seemed pleased enough not to be venturing into a house containing two corpses.

There were various pairs of boots and shoes to choose from and Bennett collected them all and took them over to where Bella and her mother were waiting. It was plain that neither of the women had ever had to wear second-hand footwear before and looked as though the very notion made them feel ill. At length, they overcame their repugnance and to

Bennett's relief, it chanced that the dead man's boots were a good enough fit for Mrs Lowry, while the woman's shoes could have been tailor-made for Bella.

There was nothing stylish or fancy about their new shoes, but it looked to Bennett as though they would do very nicely. Propping the scattergun in a corner of the school-room, he went back to the house to see if he might be able to root out some food to top up their depleted stocks.

It has to be said that Will Bennett was very far from being the most squeamish of individuals, but even he found it a little unnerving, ransacking the closets in the kitchen in the presence of the previous owners of the foodstuffs he was taking. Lord, he thought to himself, I hope I'm not growing superstitious as I get older. After he had collected some cornpone, oatmeal and one or two other comestibles, Bennett thought that he could perhaps do with a breath of air. Just as this idea struck him, he heard the sound of horses' hoofs and by the time he was out of the house, the Lowrys too had left the school-house and come out to see who it might be.

Over the years of war and the time after that, that he had spent drifting up and down the country, Will Bennett prided himself that he had grown to be a pretty good judge of character. He did not care one little bit for the look of the four men who had ridden up to the mission and were now sitting on their horses, watching him and the two women without speaking. Unless I'm much mistook, thought Bennett, I'm looking now at the ones who killed the missioners in the kitchen.

It was difficult to say which of the four riders was the more ill-favoured. One was pretty obviously a Mexican. He had a face that was both sensuous and fleshy, but with eyes set in that face which were as cold and expressionless as glass beads. The man next to him was very young, but looked to Bennett to have a mean, cruel look about him; like the sort of vicious boy who delights in pulling the wings off flies. The two others might have been brothers, so similar were they in appearance. Both had the air about them of men who would kill a fellow being at the drop of the proverbial hat. Bennett knew the type well enough.

The silence stretched out until Bennett said, 'Good day to you all. We were just leavin', so I hope you won't think us rude if'n we don't stop to visit with you.'

The youngest of the men had been staring at Mrs Lowry's daughter in a way that Bennett did not care for. This man said, 'Ain't she fresh and pretty? Friend of yours, mister?'

'Don't you trouble yourself about that,' said Bennett firmly, his heart sinking at the words. 'I'm takin' care of her, which is all you need know.'

'Taking care of her, huh?' said the Mexican. 'I'd surely like to take care of her too!' His companions laughed.

'I reckon that'll be just about enough of that,'

Bennett said to the men with a confidence that he was very far from feeling. 'Like I say, I'm protecting these ladies from hazard, while we make our way north.'

'You escape from somewhere?' asked one of the two men who looked like brothers. 'I see where you got a chain on your wrist. You bust out o' gaol or something?'

'I reckon that's my affair.'

'Ain't exactly the friendly type, are you?' inquired the youngest of the men. Bennett walked towards the riders, hoping to draw them away from the women. He was careful not to give any impression that he was wanting to start a fight, because with four on one, he could see straight off where that would end. Truth to tell, he didn't really know what he proposed to do, beyond moving them clear of Mrs Lowry and Bella. The men did not seem to be unduly worried by Bennett. They were all four of them too busy sizing up Bella with their eyes and Will Bennett knew that unless there was the most enormous stroke of good fortune, such as an earthquake or a bolt of lightning slaying those riders, that the young girl was in serious difficulty. Thing was, he had no idea at all what to do about it. Even if he drew his piece now and began blazing away at them, he'd be lucky to kill one before they got him. He could see that all four of them were waiting and ready for such a desperate move on his part.

As he neared the riders, so they began playing with

45

him, backing up and encircling him. They made no move to attack, but simply kept their distance, walking their horses round him. For his part, Bennett kept turning round, so that he was facing them as best he could, notwithstanding the fact that there was always at least one of them behind him. It was like some strange dance. As he moved in this way, further away from the mission, Bennett could see that the Lowrys were just standing there, making no effort to run or hide. He supposed it possible that they really didn't apprehend the danger that they were all in. Perhaps they'd never encountered men like these before.

'Why'n't you fellows just move on by and leave us be?' asked Bennett. 'It ain't much to ask.'

The men in front of him, the two who looked like brothers, adopted expressions suggestive of deep thought. For a moment, Bennett almost believed that his direct appeal had worked and they were going to leave him and the two women be. Then there was a crushing pain behind his right ear and the horizon tilted insanely. The ground whirled round and then rushed up to meet him as he crashed to the dust.

CHAPTER 4

Only gradually did the urgent voice of Mrs Lowry penetrate Bennett's consciousness. 'Mr Bennett,' she was saying loudly, 'Mr Bennett, in the name of God will you come to?' Even in the foggy and uncertain state of his mind, Bennett was a little shocked to hear a lady take the name of the Lord in vain like that. In addition to more or less shouting in his face, she was shaking him roughly, her desperate anxiety to rouse him overcoming any social niceties she might feel. At length, he opened his eyes.

'Thank the Lord!' exclaimed Mrs Lowry. 'Now will you get up and do something?'

'Do something?' repeated Bennett helplessly, 'why, what would you have me do?'

'Those men have taken my daughter. One of them jumped down and simply threw her across his saddle, like she might have been a captive of war. Then they rode off.'

'What happened to me? Was I shot?'

47

'No, one of those villains drove a rifle butt into the side of your head. You dropped like a pole-axed ox. Please get up and hurry.'

'How long've I been out for?'

'Perhaps a half hour, maybe longer. I don't rightly know, I'm plumb distracted. Do, please, get up and help.'

Despite the blow to his head, Bennett's mind felt clearer and sharper than it had done for some long while. Maybe, he thought, that shock has cured the scrambling of my brains which that minie ball accomplished at Atlanta. He laughed at the thought, causing Mrs Lowry to say sharply, 'Land sakes, why are you sitting there giggling like a schoolgirl? Will you get up and take action?'

'That I will, ma'am,' said Bennett, as he got to his feet. 'They seem not to have bothered taking my pistol from me. There's a horse in yonder field, which I'll endeavour to mount. Go fetch me that scattergun as I left in the school-room.'

There wasn't, from all that he was able to apprehend, time to hunt out saddle and bridle and fool around tacking up the mount. Bennett had ridden bareback often enough and since speed was of the essence, he supposed that he could do so again. The horse in the little corral by the house seemed to be a biddable enough creature and made no protest when Bennett clambered on to her back. It would be a rough journey, without even a bridle, but he thought he could guide the beast by tugging at her

48

mane. For a time, Bennett had lived and worked with a bunch of Choctaw and they had shown him various tricks of that sort. He'd do well enough.

Mrs Lowry came out of the school-room with the scattergun, holding it out gingerly at arm's length, like it might have been a venomous snake or something. As she approached, Bennett said, 'It won't bite, ma'am. You needs must cock the piece and pull the trigger, 'fore it'll do any harm. Which way did they go?'

'Back the way they came from, in that direction.'

'Well, ma'am, all I can tell you is that I'll do my very best.' Bennett reached down and took the scattergun from the frightened-looking woman. Mrs Lowry looked a deal less formidable now, in the character of an anxious mother. He added, 'Don't you worry, none. I tackled bigger game than this before now.' Then, with no more ado, he jabbed the horse in her flanks with his booted heels and they were off and away, cantering off across the dusty plain in search of the men who had taken young Bella.

With a pistol at his hip, the scattergun slung across his back and he himself heading out on horseback to face mortal danger, Will Bennett felt complete again for the first time in a good long while. The wind in his face felt good and he was young and alive. The only slight problem nagging away at him was, surprisingly, the ethics of the case.

All his life, right from his boyhood in Tennessee up to the present day, Bennett had lived by the

Rattlesnake Code. It was a simple enough set of rules and one subscribed to by many rough and dangerous men who otherwise took little heed of the laws of man or God. In essence, it amounted to this: being a real man meant never striking at another without offering a warning or challenge. Just like the rattler, which signals its displeasure and aggressive intentions with a soft shaking of the bony rings around its tail, so too should the man of honour always give an opponent the opportunity to defend himself. There must be no attacking from behind, no ambush killings, nor any skulking in the shadows to take a shot at a man without warning. You cannot smile at man or break bread with him and then kill him.

The exceptions to this are when a fight has already begun and you are pursuing a man who knows of your intentions to kill him. Under those circumstances, it is considered permissible to lay in wait and ambush a man. It is thought that if both parties already know that they are up against each other, then it is for each of them to take care. As long as they are forewarned of attack, anything is fair.

Thinking the matter over as he rode, Bennett came to the conclusion that this was really a case of pursuit. Those bastards had knocked him out cold and made off with a lady under his protection. They must surely be aware that they had set off the powder train and that the man so treated was apt to come looking for vengeance. If they didn't know that, then they had no business being on the scout like this in the territories.

The plain stretched out before him; bleak, barren and featureless. The only thing to vary the blank monotony of the landscape was a slight undulation in the distance, which was a low hill covered with scrubby pines. Bennett reined in and thought things over for a minute or so. There was no cover anywhere else and if Mrs Lowry was right and those four men only had a half hour start on him, then he should be able to see, at the very least, the dust that they were kicking up. There was nothing; not a trace of them. The only place that they could possibly have concealed themselves was that wood.

A sickening realization came to Bennett and that was that they could only have abducted Mrs Lowry's daughter for some carnal and dishonourable purpose. They'd be compelled to dismount and most likely all lend a hand if they wished to fulfil those lusts. Where better than behind some trees, out of sight of anybody who might be passing. Will Bennett was that angry that he could hear the blood singing in his head as it pulsed through. He could not recollect the last time that he had been consumed by such a murderous, killing rage as this. If he was going to be able to rescue that poor girl, then he would have to put her out of his mind and plan this business in a more objective fashion, like he would have done a minor skirmish during the late war.

Starting towards the wooded slope at a more sedate pace, one aspect of the business was still puzzling

Bennett and that was why the men hadn't just killed him, or at the very least deprived him of his gun. The most likely explanation as far as he could see was that they had taken him for a fellow outlaw and wished to let him be as far as possible. Taking the girl had been one thing; shooting him down like a dog, something else again. They would have done better to kill me, though Bennett grimly. Because by God, either I or they will die this day.

Having, to the best of his ability, put all thoughts of the innocent girl who might at that very moment be being ravished by those beasts, Bennett turned over in his mind the best way of approaching the situation. As he came nearer to the woods, he knew that it would be no good hurrying things. If any of those men heard the drumming of hoof beats, they would at once be on their guard and that would be fatal; not just for him, but also for the girl. His only hope lay in complete surprise. He had been travelling at a trot, but as he reached the tree line, Bennett slowed the mare right down until she was walking at a sedate pace, picking her way delicately through the pine cones and leaves that littered the forest floor.

There were four of them; Bennett had faced worse odds than that during the War Between the States and still come out ahead of the game. He had what he always thought of as his ace in the hole, the edge that all good gunmen and killers require if they are to live long. It was that he never hesitated for the merest fraction of a second when once he had decided upon his course of action. When you were riding down upon a heavily armed enemy, the tiniest delay could prove lethal and result in your own death, rather than that of the man you were attacking. For Will Bennett, it was enough to reason the thing out in his mind beforehand and figure out if he was justified in his actions and behaving in accordance with his conscience. If that was so, then he saw no purpose in pausing or agonizing about pulling the trigger or slashing with his knife. To some, this seemed to be a form of ruthlessness, but it was in reality the exact opposite. Bennett was a man who had to know that he was acting correctly, at least in his own lights. That being the case, he felt free to strike as swiftly as a rattler.

Ahead, he could hear noises. He halted the mare and listened intently. There was the sound of scuffling and a few curses. Then there was a despairing little scream; obviously from the girl. Bennett took the scattergun from his back and cocked both hammers. Then he drew the Colt Navy from its holster and cocked that as well with his thumb. For a moment, he was undecided about which of the weapons he should have in his right hand and which in his left. Since he might need to undertake some accurate shooting and this was not an occasion that just throwing a lot of lead around would answer, he kept the pistol in his right hand and held the scattergun loosely at his hip. He was keenly aware that there was an innocent person among those he hoped to kill and that would make this little foray a tricky enterprise.

Walking the horse forward, slowly and cautiously, Bennett reached a point at which the noises were supplemented by glimpses of movement between the trees ahead. Those engaged in this lively activity were plainly too engrossed in their own affairs to pay any heed to anything else. They hadn't thought it necessary to post a sentry or to take turns in whatever they were up to. Bennett shook his head, with the trained soldier's almost puritanical disapproval of the sloppy ways of civilians. Still and all, there was no further call for delay and so Bennett kicked his horse as hard as he could, which caused her to bolt forward, almost unseating him. He clung on to her mane and leaned as low as he could, so as not to present any sort of target to the men upon whom he was now riding down at a gallop.

It was little short of a miracle that Bennett succeeded in staying on his mount as she thundered through the trees to the little clearing. He had a brief, confused vision of the struggling group, all turned towards him, taken aback by his sudden emergence on to the scene. One man was standing apart from the others and Bennett shot him at once with the pistol. He only wanted to use the scattergun when he was perfectly sure that the girl was clear of his field of fire. As soon as he had fired, Bennett yanked as hard as he could on the mane, causing the mare to swerve round and rear up in terror. The other three men had thrust the girl from them and were diving for their weapons. One of the men he had pegged earlier as being one of two brothers was handicapped by having his pants around his ankles. Bennett fired twice with the pistol and then saw that it was the perfect time to use the scattergun. The young man who he had seen back at the mission station was actually naked from the waist down. Having apparently removed his pants entirely, he was now running across the glade, presumably to where he had left his clothes. Bennett felt no compunction about blasting this wretch in the back with the scattergun. He didn't fall at once and so Bennett let him have the second barrel too, which had the desired effect.

Three down and only one to go. Will Bennett was feeling that sheer exhilaration which only the heat of battle had ever given him. He was so pleased that perhaps his attention lapsed momentarily. Which would go some way towards explaining why the surviving member of the gang that had abducted the girl was able to get off a shot which nearly killed the man on horseback. If the mare hadn't jittered sideways at that precise moment, it would have been all up with Bennett. As it was, he felt a searing pain in the bicep, as though somebody had touched him with a red-hot poker. The agony focused his mind, snapping him out of the reverie of triumph into which he had almost fallen. His response was swift and deadly. Before the man could get off another shot, Bennett fired twice, hitting the fellow in the chest with both shots.

There was a deathly hush in the little clearing after the shooting ended. It had all taken no more than a few seconds and four men lay dead. Ignoring the burning pain in his left arm, Bennett averted his eyes, so as not to acknowledge that the girl's clothes were in a state of disarray and said, 'I'm sorry I couldn't get here any sooner, Miss Bella.'

Despite the fact that she had received the most devastating shock of an attempted rape, followed by seeing four men killed in front of her, Arabella Lowry seemed to be remarkably self-possessed. She said, 'Oh, you're hurt.'

'I've had a lot worse and lived to tell the tale. Did you . . . I mean did they. . . ?'

'No,' she said shortly, 'but it wasn't for want of trying. Let me make myself decent and then tend to your arm.'

'Lord almighty, Miss Bella, never mind about that now. I'd feel happy to leave this spot just as soon as we are able. God knows who might be drawn by the noise of all that gunfire. It sounded like a regular battle.'

'There, I'm quite ready now,' said Bella. 'Why don't you hop down and let me have a look at your wound?'

'Can you ride?' asked Bennett abruptly.

'I have done. Why?'

'I don't kind o' take to the notion of riding bareback

any more today. I'm thinking that if we took the horses of those wretches, it might make for an easier trip out of the Indian Nations and back into civilization. Can your ma ride too?'

'She rides well enough.'

'Then let's get from here as soon as we are able,' said Bennett.

Together, the two of them went over and chose the three of the four horses which looked to Bennett to be suitable for beginners. He removed the tack from the remaining horse and turned it loose along with the mare he had taken from the mission station. Then, while Bella waited out of sight, he set about despoiling the dead, taking three pistols and also a flask of powder and some balls. When he rejoined the girl, he said, 'You and your ma could do worse than keep these pistols along of you. Nothing to discourage some beast intent upon having his way with you than seeing a thirty-six Navy pointing at his belly.'

'Your arm is all over blood, Mr Bennett. Will you not let me do something about it?'

'Not yet. I'd feel a lot better if we were away from this place now. Can you mount up by yourself or may I lend you a hand?'

Arabella Lowry blushed. 'The truth is, there is a mounting-block where I ride at home and a groom to help.'

'Well I'd doubt you'll find either a mounting-block or a groom hereabouts, but I'm happy to help.'

Bennett thought a moment and then said, 'You've rode astraddle, I suppose? Not just side-saddle?'

Once again, the girl reddened, embarrassed to appear in his eyes as so incapable. She said, 'I haven't ridden other than side-saddle since I was little.'

'Well, now's the time. Look, I'll lock my hands together here and you can use that as a step to get up on to the stirrup. Wait while I shorten those stirrup leathers, though.'

After he had adjusted the saddle to his liking, Bennett clasped his hands and invited the girl to use him as her own, personal mounting-block. Her long skirts and petticoats made it hard for her to sit on the horse properly and Bennett clucked with ill-disguised irritation. He said, 'I'd suggest that you change into one of those dead men's pants 'til we get back to the mission, only I'm afraid you'd faint from shock.'

'I can manage like this, thank you.'

'Well, if you say so,' Bennett muttered dubiously. 'And now let's make tracks. All else apart, your ma will be struck all of a heap with worry by this time.'

It was no easy matter with his injured arm for Bennett to ride his own horse and lead a spare mount along too. All the while he was doing this, he also had to set a watch upon the girl and make sure that she wasn't about to topple off her horse. All in all, he was mightily glad when they got back to where Bella's mother was pacing up and down distractedly. When she saw them coming, Mrs Lowry ran to meet her daughter, crying, 'Oh, thank God! I never thought to set eyes upon you again.'

Somehow, Arabella Lowry tumbled down from the saddle and into her mother's arms and there followed a protracted spell of weeping and feminine conversation of the sort that always left Will Bennett at a loss to know where to look. At last, Bella said, 'Mama, we must dress Mr Bennett's arm. He's been shot.'

'It's nothing at all to speak of, ma'am,' said Bennett hastily. 'I beg that you don't concern yourself none over it. I had worse than this many a time.' His sleeve was now drenched in blood, though, and Mrs Lowry insisted that he dismount so that she could see what, if anything, she and her daughter could do.

As he had said, the wound was not a deep one, consisting only of a furrow or groove across the outer part of his left bicep, but the ball had obviously opened a vein, because the bleeding showed no sign of stopping. 'I need to rest up, at least for a day,' said Bennett. 'It's a damned nuisance.' Then, recollecting himself, he said hurriedly, 'I beg your pardon, ladies. It just slipped out.'

'Never mind about that,' replied Mrs Lowry, 'what do you suggest?'

'I don't know how you and your daughter feel, but it wouldn't set right with me to stay in that house, belonging to those dead folk. Nor wouldn't I find it respectful to snore away in a church. Which leaves the school-room.'

'You're right, of course. How shall we arrange matters?'

'First off is where we need to untack these critters and turn them out to graze. Miss Bella, do you think you can unbuckle everything and take off the saddles and bridles?'

'I'm sure I can,' said the girl stoutly, although she quaked inwardly at the thought of getting so intimately acquainted with three horses.

'As for you, ma'am,' Bennett said to Mrs Lowry, 'you think as you could move these bags and packs into the school?'

'Of course I can. Just sit there quietly, sir. You've already done more than anybody could have hoped. I'm forever in your debt.'

Will Bennett shrugged and said, 'That's nothing to the purpose. We ain't out o' the woods yet.'

CHAPTER 5

Under Bennett's direction, Mrs Lowry and her daughter bound up his wounded arm tightly and he now lay flat on his back on the floor of the school-room. He gathered that Bella had eventually got the horses free of their tack and turned them out. When she came back from the field he said, 'Well, Miss Bella, you did all right without a groom.'

'I hope you're not teasing me, Mr Bennett?' she replied with a smile.

'Lord forbid that I should take such a liberty.'

At that moment, Mrs Lowry returned. She had, unbidden, entered the house of the dead missioners and brought down from upstairs some blankets and bolsters. Bennett was hugely impressed, saying, 'Why, ma'am, you're becoming a regular looter. We'll make a guerrilla of you yet.'

There was little to eat, other than cornpone and some cold vegetables. Bennett absolutely flat forbade any thought of kindling a fire; either for cooking or to provide a little cheery warmth. Instead, the three of them sat or lay in the school-room. Mrs Lowry asked the wounded man what had brought him to his present pass. 'Would you consider it an impertinence, Mr Bennett, were I to inquire how come you have been drifting across the country without settling down at all? The war's been over these three years and more.'

It was, astonishing to relate, the first time in the last three years that anybody had asked this question directly of Will Bennett. He thought it over for a while and then, when Mrs Lowry was beginning to think that she had been too inquisitive and had offended the man, he said, 'I was only seventeen when I joined up. Right after Fort Sumter, you know. If it hadn't o' been for the war, I'd o' most likely just worked on my pa's smallholding and then when he died, carried on there by myself. But off I went and for four years, I fought all over the place. By the time it all ended, I was twenty-one years of age and hadn't known any steadiness in my life since I was nigh on a boy.'

Bennett stopped and looked thoughtful. He was unused to speaking at such length about himself and it made him feel a little uneasy. He continued, 'Somehow, me and a bunch of others just couldn't settle down and live like we had 'fore the war. I couldn't bear the thought o' spending my days digging and ploughing like my pa, breaking my back in hard labour, just to put a little food on the table. No ma'am, it wasn't to be thought of. Anyway, by the time I got home, I found my pa was dead anyway and the whole place overgrown. So I just set out like I'd done during the war. Spent some time here, a little spell there. A bit of digging, tending livestock, working in a bar-room. 'Fore I knowed it, three years had passed and here I am.' He looked at the two women who were staring at him with a rapt expression on their faces and said, 'Lordy, that's about enough 'bout me. Let's talk of somethin' else, I beg of you.'

They all slept early, almost as soon as dusk fell. Bennett lay at one end of the school-room; Bella and her mother at the other. It wasn't precisely how a book of polite behaviour would have set out the sleeping arrangements, perhaps, but then they weren't in some drawing room in Boston.

As soon as he woke the following morning, Bennett knew that his arm was going to be fine and that the wound wasn't infected. This was a great relief to him, although he hadn't mentioned the possibility of blood poisoning or anything of that nature to the women. At any rate, his arm was not throbbing, nor did it feel hot to the touch and he himself was not burning up with some fever. All in all, things looked like they were going to work out just fine. He went outside to answer a call of nature and then stood there afterwards, just admiring the dawn. He didn't hear Arabella Lowry come up behind him. She startled him by observing, 'It surely is a lovely morning.'

'It is that,' he replied. Then he noticed that she had nothing on her feet and said, 'Lord, you'll catch your death o' cold. Whyn't you go back inside and put something on your feet?'

'Don't fuss,' she said, 'you sound like my mother.'

They stood there for a while in companionable silence, until the girl asked, 'What will you do when once you get us to safety?'

'Tell you the truth, miss, I ain't thought on that yet. I'm sure things will work out. Don't you fret about me. I'm used to taking care o' my own self.'

At that moment, Mrs Lowry came out and called out to her daughter. 'Arabella Lowry, have you taken leave of your senses? Why are you walking about in this chilly air without a stitch on your feet? If you don't catch the pneumonia, then I'm a Dutchman. Get right in there and put on your shoes.' She couldn't for the life of her imagine why this sensible advice should cause both Mr Bennett and her daughter to burst out laughing.

Mrs Lowry proved to be a pretty competent horse-woman; somewhat better at any rate than her daughter. The three of them rode north at a fairly leisurely pace, which, according to Bennett was likely to bring them out of the Indian Nations and into Kansas after perhaps another day or two. He said to Mrs Lowry, 'Trotting along like this is well and good, but we'd make better progress were we to alternate it with cantering. You able to oblige?'

'I have no difficulty cantering, Mr Bennett,' she

replied. 'I was raised with horses. I could ride before I could walk.'

'No, but really?' he said in amazement. 'How come? You don't strike me much like a farmer's daughter, if you'll forgive me saying so.'

'Farmer's daughter?' She gave a short bark of laughter. 'You're an impudent young fellow. Of course my father wasn't a farmer. He bred racehorses as a hobby. It's a long tale, but the end of it is that I'll take oath that I can ride as well as you, for all that you spent those years in the army.'

'I might be able to canter a little,' said Arabella doubtfully, 'but I've done more dressage than I have hacking out.'

'Well let's give it a try,' said Bennett and dug his heels into the horse's flanks. Mrs Lowry was after him in an instant and her daughter was left to bring up the rear.

Will Bennett and Mrs Lowry sailed across the sparse, scrubby grassland as though they had been born to this mode of travel while Arabella lagged further and further behind. In the end, it was Bennett, rather than her mother, who suggested that they should slow down for a bit and give the girl a chance to catch up with them. They did so and as her daughter came within hailing distance, Mrs Lowry turned in the saddle and called back to her, 'Come along, child, don't be such a slowpoke!'

At this, Bennett laughed out loud for the first time since they had encountered each other back in the stage. 'What's so amusing, sir?' asked Mrs Lowry.

'Oh, I didn't mean to cause any offence, ma'am,' replied Bennett, 'it's just that you seem like a different person in the saddle. Not so . . .'

'Stuffy?' she suggested.

'It's not the word I would o' chosen,' he said tactfully, 'but yes, something of the sort.'

After they had continued for another ten miles or so, by which time Bella was expressing her desire for a rest, Bennett saw in the distance a building of some sort. They were on a high ridge of land and the building was some two or three miles ahead. It was surrounded by a patchwork quilt of fields. 'Some kind of farm, by the look of it,' said Bennett.

'What do you advise, Mr Bennett?' asked Mrs Lowry. 'We carry on and pass close by or skirt around it?'

' 'Less I'm mistook, ma'am, that's goin' to be white folks living there. I don't see Chickasaw or Choctaw building something like that. I should say we might at least be able to rest up there. Only the most inhospitable man in the world would turn away such travellers as you and your daughter.'

As they neared the farm, it could be seen that the farmhouse itself was built of logs. It was a stout, well-constructed place, which looked to Bennett's eye as though it had been so situated as to be defensible in times of hostility. Which, if this was indeed a white man living in the heart of the Indian Nations, was a sensible precaution. One curious circumstance was that the three or four men he could see toiling in the fields looked to be Indians. This was a strange setup and he was curious to know what lay behind it.

The three riders reined in a hundred yards from the odd-looking house. Bennett said, 'Happen I should go forward first and see who lives here and that everything's all right.' At that moment, the door opened and a tall, muscular-looking man in late middle age strode out of the house and headed towards them. This individual had a bushy black beard which tumbled over his chest like a waterfall. His face was pleasant and rugged and he put Bennett in mind of the mountain men with whom he had fought side by side in the war.

'Well met, strangers,' said the man when he was near enough to speak without raising his voice over-much. 'It sure is good to have visitors. You'll set a while with me and my family, I hope?'

'That's right neighbourly of you, sir. . .' began Bennett and almost immediately a broad grin split the man's face and he said;

'I'll lay any odds you're from Tennessee. Am I right?'

'That you are, sir. Born and raised.'

'Well, that makes two of us. Would these charming ladies be kin to you?'

To Bennett's unutterable surprise, Mrs Lowry said at this point, 'Mr William Bennett here isn't related to us by blood, but he's looked after us better than I could have expected my own brother to do.'

'Looked after you, has he?' said the man, 'that makes good listening. Anyways, my name is Nathaniel Gold and this here's my farm. You are very welcome.'

'I'm Mrs Lowry and this is my daughter, Arabella.'

'Though everybody calls me Bella,' the girl put in at this point.

'Bella and Mrs Lowry it shall be then. I hope you'll all call me Nathaniel. It's a good long while since anybody's addressed me as Mr Gold and to tell you the truth, it'd make me nervous.'

'Nathaniel, it is,' said Mrs Lowry. The more time he spent in her company, the less starchy and intimidating Mrs Lowry seemed to Will Bennett. In fact since mounting the horse that day, she had appeared to be positively human.

They dismounted and led the horses towards Nathaniel's home. A woman came out to greet them; a Choctaw squaw. 'My wife,' said Nathaniel Gold, without a trace of embarrassment, 'the usefullest wife a man ever had. My dear, greet our guests.' His wife smiled shyly, but said nothing. He explained, 'She ain't a regular whale on English, but that don't signify.'

The house was larger than it appeared to be from outside. Although consisting of only a single storey, it stretched back for some distance, which had not been obvious when they were approaching it. Nathaniel Gold took it for granted that they would be staying for some little while and so, after leaving

Mrs Lowry and her daughter in the keeping of his wife, he invited Bennett to come and untack the horses and turn them out.

As the two of them unbuckled the girths and removed the bridles, the owner of the farm reached out his hand and touched the handcuffs dangling from Bennett's right wrist. He said, 'I have a good saw that'll remove that with no difficulty. Let's go over to the barn when we've dealt with these animals.'

There was a vast array of tools and farm implements in the barn. Nathaniel Gold chose a narrow-bladed saw of a curious design that Bennett had never seen before; the blade held under tension in a metal frame. 'Come over here to the anvil,' said Gold, 'I'll need you to hold the thing steady with your other hand.'

Together, the two men managed to remove the handcuffs, first by sawing through the section around Bennett's wrist and then by prising it apart with a chisel. He rubbed his wrist appreciatively and said, 'That feels good, having my wrist free again.' The man called Nathaniel said nothing, but just smiled. 'You ain't asked how I come to have such a thing on me,' said Bennett. 'You're not curious?'

'Not overly. It's not my affair. You want to tell me about it, I figure you will.'

Upon which, Bennett thought it would be churlish not to repay such a good deed with at least some slight account of the events which led to his being handcuffed to a federal marshal. Then, because Nathaniel was such a good listener, he continued talking until he had told him the whole story about how he had looked after and cared for Mrs Lowry and her daughter.

When he had finished, Nathaniel Gold looked at him for a second or two, before saying, 'You're a study, son. Let's see what's cooking in the kitchen.'

Onatima, which was what Gold's wife was named, had been getting acquainted with the Lowrys and the three women were working together amicably in the spacious kitchen. Never had Bennett been to such a home, where strangers like him, Mrs Lowry and Bella fitted right in and felt at home at once. When the meal was almost ready, Onatima went outside and gave a warbling call which carried for a half mile out across the fields. By the time the food was set on the table, which was an exceedingly large one, four Indian youths had entered the house, laughing and talking. They turned out to be Gold's sons and they were as good-natured, honest and openhearted as their father.

The talk at table was general, covering the weather, the agricultural prospects for that year's harvest and the desirability of buying some hogs. The young men asked no questions of Bennett or his companions and he had the impression that having travellers and wanderers invited to their meals was a far from uncommon experience for the boys.

After they had eaten and his sons had returned to

their work, Gold led Will Bennett outside while the women tidied up. Once they were clear of the house, Gold lit a pipe and smoked contentedly for a while, before saying, 'You've had a tough time of it lately, if what you say is true.'

'It's nothing. I had worse, especially during the war.'

'You know, we're only a short ride from a post halt for that stage to Kansas. We could deliver those two ladies there tomorrow and they could pick up their journey where they left off.'

Bennett's face lit up with pleasure. 'You don't say so? That's just fine. If you can point us in the right direction, I'll take them there now and we'll see about catching the stage tomorrow.'

Nathaniel Gold said nothing for a time and just carried on puffing at his pipe. Then he remarked, 'You won't need to see them all the way back to their home, maybe. I like what I see of you, Bennett. I've a notion a man like you would be an asset to me here. Those boys of mine are handy enough, but it would be a treat to have another fellow from Tennessee to work with and talk to. What do you say?'

'I say that's real nice of you, sir,' said Bennett, touched beyond measure by the offer, 'but I'm afraid it won't do.'

'Won't do? How so?'

'I kind o' promised to take care of Mrs Lowry and her daughter. I can't run out on 'em now. Even gettin' 'em on the stage won't be any guarantee of them getting safely home.'

'You've been convicted of murder and you'd still run the chance of being caught and hanged, just to be sure those folk got home safe? Like I say, Bennett, you're a rare study.'

'I wouldn't sleep easy if I abandoned them now,' said Bennett apologetically. 'I think they've kind of grown to rely on me. It'd be a right scurvy trick to cut and run now.'

It was made very clear to Bennett and the Lowrys that it would cause great offence if they were to decline the offer of accommodation that night. In the morning, Gold said that he would drive them himself to the post where they could pick up the stage north. The horses they could leave with him and if they later wanted to take them back again, well, that was fine with him.

In all his wandering since the war had ended, Bennett did not recall ever being in a more agree-able home. Nathaniel Gold enjoyed having visitors and from little things that had slipped out, it appeared that sometimes this became a cause of slight friction between him and his wife. During the meal that evening, to Bennett's annoyance, Gold mentioned that he had tried to lure him into staying on and working with him and that the man had refused because he felt an obligation to Bella Lowry and her mother. Both the Lowrys looked at him in amazement upon hearing this. To his consternation, Bella's eyes had a glittery look about them which suggested that she might have been moved to tears.

After the meal, Bennett announced that he wished to go for a stroll alone. He left the house and wandered away, past the fields and up towards the hills surrounding Nathaniel Gold's farm. He sat down on a rock and began thinking matters through in his slow, patient and methodical fashion, when he saw a figure emerge from the house and start heading his way. He could see that it was a woman and the long, flowing hair told him that it must be Bella Lowry, rather than her mother. Bennett clucked in irritation.

When the young woman came up to where he was sitting, Will Bennett rose courteously to his feet, but Bella said, 'Oh please don't get up, Mr Bennett.' She sat on a neighbouring rock and began unburdening herself.

'I was just so distressed when I thought that my mother and I were going to go off tomorrow and never set eyes on you again. I'm so glad that you're coming all the way home with us.'

'Well, Miss Bella, I reckon it to be my duty. I'm sure you've no occasion to mention it.'

'Oh, please don't keep calling me "Miss Bella"! You don't have to be so formal with me.'

'I'm sorry, it seems to come natural.'

'Wouldn't you have been sorry to part, if we went off tomorrow and never saw each other again?'

It was at this point that it struck Will Bennett like a thunderbolt from a clear blue sky that this respectable young girl was actually sweet on him! The realization was so shocking that for a moment he was dumbfounded and rendered quite incapable of speech. And yet, was it as unforeseen as all that? He was only twenty-four years of age and she was what, seventeen or eighteen? It wasn't, perhaps, unthinkable. As all this was rushing through his mind, Bella Lowry said, 'Well?'

'Well?' he repeated stupidly.

'I asked if you would be sorry if we never met again after tomorrow.'

Bennett was saved from the need to answer this awkward and unlooked for inquiry, when the door to the farmhouse opened and Mrs Lowry came out, obviously looking for her daughter. The girl at his side said urgently, 'Don't say anything to my mother!' Then she jumped up and began hurrying down the slope.

CHAPTER 6

Nathaniel Gold was as good as his word and transported Bennett and the Lowrys to the staging post the next day. Bennett had been a little anxious as to how the stage might be paid for, but it transpired that Mrs Lowry never travelled anywhere without sewing a number of gold coins into her clothing, where they would not be found. She was confident of having enough to cover the journey to Burfield.

The three travellers parted from the farmer whose hospitality had been so generous and unstinting with many expressions of good will. As he shook hands with Bennett, Gold said quietly, 'When once you have seen those good people safe to their destination, think on what I said. You'd be very welcome back.'

'I truly appreciate that,' answered Bennett sincerely.

Bennett and Arabella Lowry had hardly exchanged a word that morning. On Bennett's part, this was born of a natural delicacy; what motivated the girl, he was quite unable to say. Had she repented of expressing her feelings the evening before? He had no idea, but was glad that the two of them had scarcely been alone since then.

By great good fortune, there were only three passengers in the stage from Sherman and there was no difficulty about purchasing tickets through to Burfield. Bennett felt a little mean about not having the money to pay for his own ticket, but Mrs Lowry seemed pleased to have his companionship and brushed aside his thanks, saying, 'Lord, sir, you've given us a good deal more than the cost of a stage-coach ride. I'll hear no more about it.'

When the stage finally drew into Burfield, the better part of forty-eight hours after they had boarded it, Bennett reckoned that they would all three of them be glad to part company for good that day. Having come this far and ensured the safety of the Lowrys, he thought that he might as well finish his self-appointed task and see them to their home. What he would then do wasn't clear to him, but he'd no doubt that something would turn up; it always did.

Bennett had left the scattergun at Gold's farm and carried only the pistol in his holster and the other two which he had taken from the dead outlaws. These he carried in his bag, out of sight. As he escorted the two women along the busy streets of Burfield, he observed in a conversational tone, 'I should think that the two of you will be right pleased to get back home.' Bella shrugged indifferently, but her mother said:

'You may well say so, Mr Bennett. I only hope my husband hasn't been too alarmed by our delay in returning. We're some days later than he might have expected.'

They were passing the grandest house that Bennett had yet seen in the town, a veritable mansion set in enormous grounds. To his immense surprise, Mrs Lowry turned in at the gate of this impressive abode, remarking casually, 'It surely is good to be home.'

Bennett stopped dead in his tracks, gazing at the imposing great house. It looked more like something one might see in Charleston or Atlanta, rather than a little backwater like this in Kansas. He said, 'Don't tell me this is where you live, Mrs Lowry?'

'That's right. What ails you?'

'It's a mite bigger than I expected, for one thing.'

'That's nothing. Come along, I know my husband will be eager to meet you.'

'Oh no, ma'am,' said Bennett, moving slowly back, away from the entrance gates. 'I'm sure he won't want to see me. If it's all the same with you, I guess I'll be moving on now.'

Just then, there came a shout of joy and a young man no older than Bennett himself came haring across the lawn from the house. Bella Lowry gave a shriek of pleasure and ran to meet him. 'Tom, I missed you so much last term,' she said. 'Why didn't you write me, you beast?'

'Pa's vexed with the two of you,' said the new arrival, 'thinks that you've gone off on some vacation, spending his money Lord knows where. Seriously, where have you been? You look like vagabonds.'

'Mr Bennett,' said Bella's mother, 'allow me to introduce my son Thomas. He's almost a lawyer now, like his father. Tom, this is Mr William Bennett, who has condescended to escort us through the Indian Nations.'

The young man shot Bennett a very strange look, but stepped forward and grasped his hand readily enough, saying, 'Glad to know you, Mr Bennett.'

'You'll be a sight gladder when you know all he's done for us,' said Tom Lowry's sister. 'If it weren't for Mr Bennett, there's no telling how things might have turned out.'

While all these joyful reunions were taking place, Will Bennett was slowly trying to edge back towards the gates, while at the same time not making his intentions obvious. He had almost reached the road, when a hand was clapped upon his shoulder from behind and a man entering the drive on foot said, 'Whoa, steady on there. Walking backwards like that leads to trouble.'

'Albert!' exclaimed Mrs Lowry, at the same moment that Bella cried, 'Papa!' The two of them rushed to embrace the stern-looking man who had warned Bennett against walking backwards. He felt left out in all this fuss and had it not been for the fact that Mr Albert Lowry, a respectable-looking citizen of perhaps sixty years of age, did not once take his eyes off him, Bennett might even now have slipped silently away. As it was, once Mr Lowry had been given a broad outline of recent developments, he cut matters short to allow his wife and daughter to 'freshen up' as he put it. He then requested the favour of a few words alone with Bennett. This promised to be a trying interview.

When once they were ensconced in Judge Lowry's private study, he invited Bennett to sit and then said, 'My wife and daughter seem very much taken with you, Mr Bennett. Perhaps you'd give me your own account of the last few days?'

Without dissembling or glossing over anything, Will Bennett outlined the events which had led to his being on the stage and also what had chanced afterwards. Judge Lowry said little during this recitation, other than asking the occasional question to clarify some point or other. When Bennett had finished speaking, the judge said, 'Well that's the damnedest story I ever did hear.' He was on the verge of making some other observations, when there was a knock at the door of the study and, without waiting to be invited in, Bella's brother Thomas entered the room.

'What is it, Tom?' growled Judge Lowry. 'I'm kind of busy right now. Can it wait?'

'No sir, it can't. I've been talking to my sister and learning a little of what this fellow has done for her and my mother. I could not leave it another second without coming and thanking you in person, Mr Bennett. If there's anything I can do for you, anything at all, mind, I'd reckon it a personal favour if you'd give me the opportunity to even up the debt I owe you a little.'

All this rather took the wind out of Judge Lowry's sails. He had been about to launch into a withering cross examination of Will Bennett, with a view to exposing any weaknesses in his account, particularly as it touched upon the crime of which he had been convicted. Irritated, he said to his son, 'You're meddling in matters which don't concern you, my boy. I'll be pleased to have my study to myself, so that I might carry on with my . . . conversation with Mr Bennett here.'

Not a whit abashed, the young man chuckled and said, 'Your interrogation, you mean!' He turned to Bennett. 'Remember what I say, I'll always be ready to stand friend to you and help you in any way I am able.'

After Thomas Lowry had left the room, the judge turned to Bennett and said, 'I'll tell you what I can do for you, Bennett. You're welcome to stay here for a few days and I'll get a doctor to look at that arm of yours. Then I'm happy to make some financial provision for you and help set you on your feet somewhere. Maybe out west in California? I'm aware that I shall be compounding a felony by not handing you over to the federal gaol, but I'm not such an ungrateful dog as all that. What do you say, man, will that suit?'

'Well, sir,' said Bennett thoughtfully, 'it's a right kind offer and I truly appreciate it. But it won't answer.'

'Won't answer, hey? I should like to know why not?'

'It's like this. There was a heap of lies wrote 'bout me in the newspapers in Dallas, elsewhere, like as not. Sayin' as I was a killer and a man who did beastly things to a woman. I reckon I need to set that straight. After that stage was ambushed, I ended up with your folks and while I been tending to them, I got to thinking. I'm a-goin' to set the record straight. I go haring off to California, folks'll think I was runnin' away 'cause them stories was true. No, I guess I'm going back to the town of Innocence to get this thing cleared up. There's a man somewhere as did a dreadful thing to a kind and innocent woman and I reckon I owe it to her and also to my own self to get to the bottom of it.'

When Bennett had finished speaking, Judge Lowry stared at him in astonishment. Up to this moment he had not been absolutely sure in his own mind that the man sitting in his study was indeed the innocent victim of a miscarriage of justice. Seeing this fellow turn down the chance to flee to a distant part of the country, being furnished with the where-withal to make a fresh start, clinched the matter for him. He said, 'It's true, isn't it? You really are an innocent man!'

'That's the strength of it sir, yes.'

'Well I'm damned. I've been a lawyer for forty years and a judge for ten of those years and this is the first time yet that I met a man who was truly innocent. They do say that the age of miracles is not yet over!'

Bennett hardly knew how to respond to this and so remained silent. Lowry said, 'You'll be wanting a bath and most likely a change of clothes. My son is about the same size as you, I'm sure that he won't mind lending you one or two items of clothing.' Judge Lowry rang a bell to summon a servant. After Bennett had gone off to wash, the judge continued to sit at his massive mahogany desk, still utterly enchanted at having, after all those long years, finally met an innocent man.

At dinner that night, Will Bennett was anything but at his ease. The setting was so grand, more like a fancy hotel than a private home, and he scarcely knew which of the many spoons, forks or knives to use. Whether by chance or design, he found himself seated beside Tom Lowry, who in the most natural way imaginable guided the other young man in which cutlery to use next as course followed course in dizzying profusion.

'What's this my father tells me about you wanting to go back south to where you were arrested?' asked Tom Lowry quietly, while the others were talking of something else.

'That's right. I need to clear things up before I can

rest easy. There's a woman dead and nobody yet called to account for it. Not to mention where I been blamed for her death.'

'You really mean to go back and try to set things straight?'

Bennett looked at the other man in bewilderment. 'Yes, of course. What else?'

'Well then, I reckon that I might come with you. You'll need another pair of hands.'

'Lord, I can't ask you to do that. You got a lot more important things to be doing.'

'More important than helping in some small way to show my thanks to the man who saved the lives of my mother and sister?' asked Tom Lowry. 'No, I don't think so.'

'What'll your pa say to such a notion?'

Tom winked at him. 'Ah, I can always bring the old man round, you'll see.'

As a matter of fact, the 'old man' took a good deal more bringing round than Tom Lowry could have guessed. 'Have you quite taken leave of your senses, boy?' said Judge Lowry angrily when he heard of the scheme. 'You have your final examinations in a month. You can forget all about this.'

'Is that how much gratitude you have for the man who saved Mother and Bella?' replied Tom hotly. 'I'm grateful to Will Bennett, even if you're not.'

In the end his father came round, as Tom had known he would all along. It would be a gross exaggeration to say that the judge was happy about the whole thing, but he agreed to pay for the expenses involved. While Bennett and Tom were packing their bags, Bella's brother announced unexpectedly, 'I suppose you know that my sister is a great admirer of yours?'

To his dismay, Bennett found himself reddening. To cover his confusion, he said hastily, 'I didn't do much to admire. No more than any other man in my place would o' done.'

'I don't mean that sort of admiration. You know what I'm talking of.'

'Maybe I do and maybe I don't. It don't signify. I've done nothing to encourage her, not no how.'

'Many a man would have done.'

'Wouldn't be right,' said Bennett, 'she's so innocent, like a child almost. I couldn't take advantage of innocence; it ain't in me to do so.'

Tom Lowry stared at the other man, thinking to himself that Will Bennett was one of nature's gentlemen.

Mrs Lowry had been saying pretty much the same thing to her husband an hour or so earlier. She had remarked when they were alone together, 'For all his rough ways, I tell you that man is a gentleman at heart.'

'Yes,' said the judge, 'I'd come to a similar conclusion myself. He surely is a rarity. An innocent man and a born gentleman, all rolled up into one. I shall be sorry to see him go.'

'I hate to think of him going back to Texas and

84

being in danger of having his neck stretched. You don't think if I tried my influence on him, he'd consent to consider this California scheme afresh?'

Her husband shook his head. 'Not he. He is dead set on clearing his name and running to earth the real murderer. Not just for his own sake, you understand, but because he is angry on behalf of the dead woman and feels he owes her a debt. Like I say, he's a remarkable individual.'

Although they were naturally anxious about the enterprise, both Mrs Lowry and her daughter thought it very right and proper that Tom should go back to Texas with Bennett and try to help him untangle things. Tom was already next door to being a qualified attorney at law himself and could perhaps examine the trial record and other documents from the case.

The day came when Tom Lowry and Bennett were to travel south. Bennett rose early and went into the grounds for a constitutional before breakfast. Almost as soon as he set foot out of the door, he saw Bella. She too had come into the gardens for an early morning stroll and it later struck Bennett that she might have been hoping to encounter him.

'Good morning, Miss Bella. I hope you're well.'

'You're always so formal. You know you're as stuffy as my parents in some ways.'

'I'm sorry,' said Bennett, 'I don't mean to be unfriendly.'

'So you and Tom are off today?'

'Yes, he's been kind enough to offer me his help.'

'Will you come back again?'

Bennett said nothing, not wishing to appear to snub the girl. He liked her very much indeed, but the idea of any sort of romantic entanglement with such an innocent young thing was quite absurd. He contented himself with saying, 'I don't rightly know what will happen in Texas. Like as not they'll end up hanging me after all.'

'Oh don't joke about such a terrible thing. Aren't you afraid?'

The young man smiled and said, 'Maybe I ain't sharp enough to have the sense to be afraid.'

'If you don't come back here,' said the girl, a little wistfully, 'will you write me?'

Bennett was on sure ground now, for here was a definite promise that he could make and keep. He said, 'If they don't hang me, Bella, I'll surely write you.' It was only later that it occurred to him that this was the first time that he had simply called her 'Bella', without preceding her name with the honorific title of 'Miss'.

Before the two men left, Judge Lowry called Bennett into his study. He said, 'I won't dwell on all you have done for me, Bennett. It's enough that you have saved the lives of my wife and daughter and I am eternally in your debt. If you get this business cleared up, then come back here and I'll help set you on your feet.'

'Thank you, sir. That's right good o' you.'

Mrs Lowry's leave-taking was less formal. She embraced the astounded young man as though they had been blood relations. She said as she did so, 'I can never thank you enough.'

Bella shook Bennett's hand formally and thanked him politely for all his attentions. Just as he and Tom Lowry were leaving the house, though, she suddenly darted up to Bennett and planted a kiss on his cheek, before running off, blushing.

It was odd, passing through the Indian Nations along the same route that he and the two women had so recently travelled. Bennett carried a pistol at his hip and was constantly on the alert for any sign of trouble. The company running the stages, though, were not minded to lose another coach to road agents and had doubled up the men riding shotgun up on the roof. There were two grim-looking army veterans atop of the coach in which he and Tom Lowry were travelling and Bennett had a suspicion that these men would prove more than a match for any casual robbers who might be minded to trouble them.

For all that he was pleasant company, Bennett found there to be a touch of childlike innocence about Tom Lowry which put him in mind of his sister Bella. He and Lowry were of about the same age, but Tom's experiences in life had been very different indeed from Bennett's. He had hardly been anyway much further than a few miles from the house where he had grown up. He'd gone to college just ten miles from his parents' home and had not fought in the war. In fact, it seemed to Bennett that the war had hardly touched that corner of Kansas where the Lowrys lived. The dreadful conflict which had lasted for so long had just been something to read about in the newspapers for the Lowrys and people like them.

Despite their vastly dissimilar backgrounds, the two young men had enough in common to find each other's company agreeable. They were both fond of horses, liked a hand of cards, drank a little more whiskey than was good for them and had an eye for a pretty girl. All in all, the journey passed well enough and the two of them did not find that they grated on each other, as could easily have proved the case.

When the stage drew into Sherman, Bennett could not help but feel a little nervous, lest somebody should recognize him and call out to denounce him as an escaped murderer. The truth was, dressed in a suit of Tom Lowry's clothes and cleanly shaven as he was, nobody was likely to recognize him as the scarecrow fellow who had left Sherman chained to a federal marshal less than two weeks ago. I might just be able to do this, thought Bennett to himself; I might just!

CHAPTER 7

They booked into a tiny little commercial hotel, planning to spend a night or two there before making for Innocence. Although they'd hardly known each other a week, Bennett and Lowry fell naturally into the habit of using each other's Christian names and anybody listening to their conversation might have been convinced that they were boyhood friends.

At dinner that night, Tom said to his new friend, 'How do you want to play this? Meaning, when we get to this town, what's the best way of hunting down the real killer of this woman, Mrs Dyson?'

'I don't know that I've got that far in my thinking,' admitted Bennett. 'It's taken all this trouble and confusion so far just to get myself free and be heading back there.'

'Lordy, Will,' said the other, 'there's no manner of use our just marching down the street of that little town without a plan.'

'I know that. I thought first off is where I could kind of hang around on the edge of town and you could see what folk are saying. Maybe something's turned up since I left. I don't know, that's 'bout all I can think of.'

Tom Lowry looked dubious. 'Well, I guess it's as good an idea as any. Mind, this is a tricky business. From what you've told us, if you're recognized there, they're apt to lynch you on the spot.'

'That's so,' said Bennett. 'Trust me, I'd not forgot it.'

'You know what might be a better idea altogether? Why don't we take the stage to Dallas and then you stay there for a day or two while I make some slight investigation in Innocence itself? Less chance of your being recognized in Dallas, I should say, than in some one-horse town.'

'I don't like that notion. That'd put all the risk on your shoulders. No, I don't take to that at all.'

'Little enough risk for me,' argued Tom Lowry, 'it's you that the citizens of Innocence might want to string up, not me. Why would anybody think to harm an attorney coming to look into a possible miscarriage of justice? I'm telling you, Will, this is the way to go about things.'

It took a little while to persuade Bennett of how sensible his new friend's plan was, but eventually he saw that there was a good deal in what was being suggested.

The following day, the two of them caught the stage to Dallas. Having installed Bennett in a comfortable hotel and left him with enough money to provide for his needs for a time, Tom Lowry hired a horse and rode out to Innocence. Bennett was not happy about taking what he thought of in his own mind as 'charity', from anybody. Still, as Tom pointed out, there was no denying that Will Bennett had saved the lives of the Lowry family's women folk and if that wasn't a debt needing to be paid then he, Tom, didn't know what was!

After Tom had left for Innocence, Bennett wandered disconsolately around Dallas. He didn't think that there was much chance of anybody identifying him with the fellow who had lately been tried for rape and murder. It wasn't as though his likeness had appeared in the newspapers or anything like that. Dressed as smartly as he now was, the odds were a million to one against anybody knowing that he was that same rootless drifter who had last been seen leaving town in the company of Marshal Ebenezer Curtis.

It was while he restlessly walked the streets that Bennett almost bumped into the one man he wished at all costs to avoid; the man who could certainly have identified him and seen to it that Bennett was soon clapped back in irons. As it was, Mick Dyson hardly noticed him, merely mumbling, 'Pardon me,' as he moved to one side and carried on down the sidewalk. As for Bennett, he was almost struck down in a heap with alarm at such a close encounter. He stared after Dyson as the farmer made his way jauntily along the street.

Jauntily! There was something very odd about Dyson's appearance and for all that he did not wish to be apprehended by the authorities, Bennett turned on his heel and began trailing the man. He wasn't that long a widow and his wife had died in the most shocking circumstances and yet Mick Dyson looked as chirpy as could be. He was dressed up smartly, left a fragrance of cologne in his wake and had been carrying, of all unlikely things, a gaudy bunch of flowers. Not to mention where the fellow seemed to have a distinct spring in his step.

Mick Dyson was making his way down a narrow street which was lined with stores and saloons. As Bennett watched, the man turned and entered a hardware store. Bennett withdrew into the shadows and waited patiently to see what might develop. He was in no special hurry, because Dyson's manner and overall demeanour had awakened a terrible suspicion, one that Bennett half hoped would prove to be unfounded. A little over twenty minutes later, according to the clock in the window of the store into whose window Bennett was making a show of gazing, Mick Dyson re-emerged from the store, minus the bunch of flowers, looking even more braced with life than he had been when he entered the place. Indeed, he had the traces of a smile on his lips and as he headed back to the main commercial area, Bennett caught the sound of a cheery tune being whistled. Noting the location of the store that Dyson had visited, Will Bennett followed his late employer through the streets of Dallas.

The trail led to a smart-looking house on the edge of town. To Bennett's surprise, Dyson bounded up the steps of this pleasant little clapboard structure and opened the door with a latch key. Then he disappeared inside. He didn't wish to draw undue attention to himself by hanging around, so Bennett carried on walking past, his mind racing furiously to make some sense of what he had so far seen this day. He turned his steps back in the direction of the hardware store, wondering if there would be any clue there as to what was going on. Of one thing he was certain-sure in his own mind and that was that Mick Dyson did not at all look like a man who had recently lost his wife in a shocking murder. Why, he wasn't even wearing mourning, thought Bennett to himself.

Charlton's Hardware Store sold a range of cheap goods which were pitched at the less prosperous sector of the market. When Bennett entered the store, it didn't take him long to come up with some item that they would be sure not to stock and so would provide the pretext for beginning a conversation with the owner.

Behind the counter stood a tall woman of perhaps thirty years of age. Her hair was that vivid, flame red which one seldom encounters unless nature has been cunningly enhanced by art. In short, Bennett thought that it looked dyed. Set prominently on the counter, in a china jug, were the flowers that Mick Dyson had been carrying when he had visited not an hour since.

'Good afternoon, ma'am,' said Bennett. 'Tell me, d'you sell firearms at all? Or, as it might be, powder and shot?'

'No, you might try further down the street aways at Donovan's. He usually has one or two knocking about the place.'

'I'm obliged to you. My, those are beautiful flowers.'

'Ain't they just,' said the woman, bending over them and inhaling the smell. 'They're a regular treat.'

'From an admirer, I'll be bound,' said Bennett gallantly.

'You may well say so. I never yet knew a lady who was immune to such things.'

'I'm sure that that's true, ma'am,' said Bennett. 'Thank you for directing me to an establishment where I can obtain powder.'

'You're welcome, I'm sure.'

Even the best friends that Will Bennett had had in the past would not have described him as a deep thinker. He may not have been deep, but he was thorough enough and as he walked round Dallas, he reasoned the matter out to his own satisfaction. That the recently widowed Mick Dyson was paying court to a woman in this town was clearly a fact. There were only two possibilities, then. Either he had already been playing the part of an aspiring lover before his wife's death or he had begun after Amelia Dyson had been murdered. Neither possibility resounded precisely to Dyson's credit and both caused Bennett to think of the farmer in a new and unflattering light.

Tom Lowry found it exhilarating to be hacking out on a fine day; cantering across the countryside, instead of being cooped up in some room, studying. It took less than three hours to reach Innocence at the rate at which he was pushing his mount. As he rode, he toyed with several possible ways of broaching the subject of his visit and finally decided that keeping as near to the truth as he could was perhaps the best course of action. So it was that once he'd arrived in the little town and found a livery stable for his horse, Lowry ambled over to the nearest saloon and, finding it all but empty, began pumping the barkeep.

'Maybe you can help me,' he said, after ordering a glass of porter, 'I'm an attorney and my company have the job of examining the case of one William Bennett. I don't suppose that you could tell me anything about that?'

'Why, you don't say so? I tell you now, friend, you come to the right shop for information on that subject and no mistake.'

'You know about the people involved?'

'Know about 'em?' exclaimed the man, 'I growed up with 'em. Well, leastways, Mick and Amelia Dyson.

95

Trotter as was, meaning Mrs Dyson.'

'What was she like?' inquired Lowry curiously, genuinely wishing to get a handle on the case.

'What was she like? Pure gold, that's what. Oh, I know that's what you all'us say of a dead person, but in 'Melia's case it's no more'n the literal truth.'

'I'm guessing folks must have been a mite aggrieved when they heard about her murder?'

'That's one way o' puttin' it. That hired man up at the Dyson place was damn near lynched, I'll tell you that for nothin'.'

Tom Lowry said nothing for a space, thinking that this was the decent thing to do. After he and the barkeep had spent half a minute contemplating Mrs Amelia Dyson's virtuous nature and the shame of how she'd been killed, Lowry said, 'You've not said anything about Mr Dyson. He must have been most cut up.'

'You'd o' thought so,' said the barkeep briefly. This looked promising and so Lowry said, 'Another glass of porter, if you please. May I treat you as well?'

'That's right nice of you. I'll take a glass of rye, if I may.'

The two of them sipped their drinks appreciatively and after what he judged to be a prudent interval, Tom Lowry said, 'So was Mr Dyson greatly affected by the death of his wife? Grief-stricken and so on?'

'Not overly, if I'm to speak plainly. Oh he was raving and shouting, I'll allow, but once that fellow Bennett had been taken in charge, it's my opinion

Mick Dyson recovered pretty well. Say, where do all these questions tend? You ain't fixin' for to call me to court or aught of that nature?'

Tom Lowry laughed amiably. 'No, nothing like that. I'm just trying to build up a picture of things.'

By the time he left the saloon, Lowry had come to the conclusion that there was definitely something a little lopsided about the case. His conversations that afternoon, undertaken casually with various people in the boarding house where he had booked a room and also in the stores of Innocence, confirmed the view he was forming.

The one thing that everybody agreed upon was that Amelia Dyson had been next door to a saint and that there had been a violent and spontaneous out-pouring of anger in the town when it was discovered that she had been outraged and brutally murdered. The fact that there had been a ready-made suspect and that this man had been an outsider was perfect for all concerned. If the folk in town had had their way, then Will Bennett would just have been hanged on the nearest tree and everybody would have forgotten all about it a week later.

The final piece of the puzzle, as Lowry saw it, fell into place when he was talking to the widow Lawson, from whom he was renting room and board while he was in Innocence. Mrs Lawson remarked that evening that Michael Dyson, who she had known as a young man, was ' "a bit of a ladies" man, if you take my meaning.'

'I'm not sure if I do.'

'Well, Mick was always chasing a pretty girl when he was younger. But then, when he married Amelia Trotter, everybody thought he'd settled down. Came of his suddenly having that farm, see. Before then, he'd been hiring himself out odd times to other men and gadding off to Dallas all the time.'

'I'm sorry,' said Lowry, 'I'm not sure that I take your meaning. How did he acquire a farm?'

'Why it belonged to 'Melia's family, of course, didn't I say? They was killed in that terrible accident and shortly afterwards, Mick Dyson was paying court to her. Then they married and he was at once a big farmer.'

Back in Dallas, Will Bennett was now quite convinced that he was on the track of something solid. He had always been one to take folks at face value; at least until he had good evidence for thinking otherwise. But that a newly widowed man, and widowed under such circumstances, could now be taking bunches of flowers to some woman and behaving like somebody who had never even had a wife, was strange. Dyson's whole air was so gay and light, that nobody would ever guess that he had lost his wife only a matter of weeks ago. There was a mystery here which needed to be probed.

Incredible to relate, until this moment it had never once struck Bennett that the murder of Amelia Dyson could have been anything other than a random lust killing, which had by the sheerest chance left him as the sole suspect. Even when the dead woman's husband had given the most damning testimony against him during the trial, Will Bennett had felt no animosity towards the man, for had not his personal loss been grievous? Remembering how Dyson had been when he'd seen him an hour ago, though, the beginning of an awful doubt was creeping into Bennett's mind. Had the murder of his wife been such a terrible affliction as Dyson had represented it to be in court? Was he really bowed down with grief and barely able to carry on living? The man who had stepped so cheerfully into Charlton's Hardware Store had certainly not given that appearance.

As he walked thoughtfully along the streets of Dallas, Bennett thought hard about the business. How did his clothes come to be reeking of whiskey on the night of the murder? He had known that the killer must have splashed liquor over him while he slept, but how did the man who carried out that frenzied attack on the woman in her own kitchen know that there was a hired help sleeping in the barn? And having had his way with Mrs Dyson and then killed her, why would this man then take the time to pause in his flight to try to lay the crime at Will Bennett's door? Everything had happened so rapidly after he was arrested, that Bennett had barely had a chance to reason the matter out from this angle. Not only that, but Mick Dyson's innocence had been taken for

granted, not only by Bennett himself, but by everybody else connected with the case. Look at the
matter from a different perspective, though, and
Dyson was surely as likely to be the murderer as he
himself was. The only thing that had tilted the investigation in his direction was that Mick Dyson was
known to the people in town and he was not.

In Innocence, Tom Lowry had been coming to a
similar conclusion about the way in which Bennett
had been railroaded into the role of depraved killer.
From all that he had been able to gather, there was
not one shred of evidence against Will Bennett,
beyond the indisputable fact that he was a drifter and
unknown to the citizens of the town in which he had
fetched up. Mick Dyson might not have been the
most popular individual in Innocence, but at least he
was known. Bennett was nobody. The trial of a local
man for such an atrocious crime would have been
disturbing and perhaps uncovered various unsavoury
facts that were better left untouched. How much
more convenient if this stranger should be thought
guilty of the rape and murder. It was the neatest solution by far and even better if there was no sort of
trial, but sanguinary vengeance exacted almost
immediately upon the supposed murderer.

Lowry wondered about the psychology of the business. Did those who tried to raise a lynch mob know
that the man they wanted to hang was most likely
innocent? Did they even care? Then he remembered
the gentle man who had rescued his mother and

sister from almost certain death and he was over-come with fury at the thought of those who would set out to hang such a man, simply to save themselves the embarrassment of looking into the matter prop-erly.

What about the court in Dallas? Hadn't they both-ered to investigate the case thoroughly? With a sinking heart, Lowry recalled that men such as Will Bennett were invariably defended by the least expe-rienced and most inept attorneys in town, working on a pro bono basis. For the modest fee that such men received, it was perhaps expecting too much that they should fight hard for some hobo who every-one seemed to think was guilty as Cain of a vile crime.

Tom Lowry was brooding moodily along these lines as he walked along Main Street the day after having the conversation with Mrs Lawson about Mick Dyson's character and disposition. A small, elderly man approached him tentatively and asked, 'Say, would you be the young fellow who's staying at Mrs Lawson's?'

'I am, sir. How may I help you?'

'Well, I don't know if you can help me. It may be that the boot's on the other foot, as you might say. I hear where you're looking into that dreadful affair over at the Dyson farm?'

Lowry felt a quickening of interest. He said, 'That is so, yes. Do you know anything about it?'

'About the murder itself? No, nothing at all. But

101

you might want to know about something that happened afterwards.'

'You want that we should go somewhere a little more private to talk?' asked Lowry. 'You might not want to talk about this on the public highway.'

'Lord, no. Chatting here as we walk along won't strike anybody as strange. Just let us be closeted together and all the world and his wife will be wondering what we're discussing. No, we're fine out here. Let's just walk down to the church there.'

The two men walked along the road, heading for the edge of town. Lowry said, 'So what was it you'd like to tell me?'

'Some of us are feeling a mite uneasy about that young fellow as was tried for Amelia Dyson's murder. There's even a whisper going round that he might o' got a raw deal.'

'That what you think?'

'I don't rightly know. We were so all-fired hasty to get the business settled and somebody called to account, I reckon that that young man was something of a Godsend, if you take my meaning?'

'I do indeed,' said Tom Lowry grimly. 'I apprehend very well what you mean.'

'Truth is, had it not been for that hobo sleeping in their barn and being covered with blood, then maybe Mick Dyson would have had some explaining to do on his own account.'

'Why do you say so?'

'Why, because within two days of that Will Bennett

being sentenced to hang, Dyson was asking me to arrange the sale of the farm. Said he couldn't bear to stay there after the tragedy and needed a fresh start, far away.'

CHAPTER 8

As far as Tom Lowry was concerned, all the facts were stacking up in favour of Bennett's innocence. There did not seem to be one solid and incontrovertible piece of evidence against the man and the more that Lowry found out, the angrier he grew. Having been at law school for the last few years, he had learned a lot about the importance of the rule of law, the presumption of innocence and a dozen other high-flown and abstract ideals. It all came down to this, though: ordinary, fallible men, with their prejudices, likes and dislikes. These were the ones who sat on juries and decided the ultimate fate of poor devils like Will Bennett. If you were a loner, an outsider, a drifter or even, God forbid a Mexican or black, then the odds were so heavily against you to begin with that you would have to be exceedingly lucky to walk free from the courtroom.

It was time to team up again with Bennett and try to decide what to do next. Even with what he had heard in Innocence, it seemed to Lowry that the wanted man would be very ill-advised to come back to the town just at the moment. The very fact that some people were starting to wonder if they had done the right thing made the situation even more delicate. Nobody likes to have it demonstrated to them that they have been hasty and unjust in their judgements. The neatest solution to this puzzle would still be the swift death of the man upon whom the crime had already been pinned. Lowry wasn't at all sure that a lynch mob might not finish off the job if Will Bennett were to show his face on the streets of Innocence right now.

The telegram that Tom Lowry sent to Dallas was unremarkable and neutral; simply announcing that TL would meet WB at the railroad depot at a certain time two days from then. Bennett was checking at the telegraph office in Dallas every evening for any messages sent *poste restante* in his agreed pseudonym. Mrs Lawson was sorry to hear that her lodger was not staying in town more than a few days. She said, 'It's been right nice, having somebody from out the area staying here. Small towns like ours, you get to feel sometimes like you're living cramped up in a little box, you know what I mean?'

'I think I do, ma'am,' said Lowry. 'Perhaps you need a little fresh air to come in from time to time, blow away unwholesome airs.'

'That is just what I was thinking myself,' she exclaimed. 'We need outsiders to come in and show us how the rest of the world is living.'

Tom Lowry arrived in Dallas earlier than he had expected and, having a little time to kill before meeting up with Bennett, decided to take a turn round town. It struck him that he could check at the telegraph office himself and see if there were any messages waiting for him from his family. No artifice or codes were needed for this purpose and he asked outright of the clerk if there were any telegrams waiting there for Tom Lowry. 'No sir,' said the man, after ferreting around in a wooden cabinet, 'nary a one.'

'Lowry, hey?' said a voice behind Tom Lowry and he turned to face an imposing-looking individual in early middle age. This man was dressed in a dark suit and had a gleaming silver star pinned to his jacket. He said, 'No relation to Judge Lowry, up in Burfield, I suppose?'

'Yes, I'm his son.'

'Well now,' said the man, 'isn't that the most astonishing coincidence? I never heard the like. Assuming it is a coincidence, that is to say.' He stretched out his hand and said, 'Sheriff Carver. I'm very glad to make your acquaintance, Mr Lowry. I wonder if we might have a few words together, if you could spare me the time?'

'Of course, Sheriff. I don't believe we've met before?'

'No, I don't recall that we have. I've had dealings with your father, though, in the past. Then he wired me a few days ago. Now I stumble across his son. You didn't say what you were doing in these parts I think, Mr Lowry.'

'I've almost finished my studies to become an attorney. I'm taking a vacation.'

'Not here on business for your pa, I suppose?'

'Sheriff, maybe you could tell me what this is all about, because you're losing me.'

'Would you care to take a walk with me to my office? We can talk more easily there.'

The two men strolled together, Sheriff Carver not intending to say anything more on the open streets. As for Tom Lowry, he was worried about Bennett. How much did this sheriff know? Was he aware that the escaped 'murderer' was even now in his town? Lowry hoped fervently that this was not the case.

When they reached the sheriff's office, Carver unlocked the door and ushered Tom Lowry inside. 'Coffee?' he asked.

'Please.'

When the two men were settled on either side of a large desk, Sheriff Carver said, 'Gave me quite a shock, I can tell you. Here we are, been watching a fellow for better than half a year and then, when we're nearly ready to pounce, I get a wire from your father. Asking a lot of questions about the very man I've had under observation. Then, before you know it, I bump into the judge's own son in town. That's some coincidence, wouldn't you say?'

Carver didn't seem to be in the least annoyed or

upset. He just sat there smiling amiably across the table at Lowry, waiting for the younger man to offer some sort of explanation of this curious state of affairs.

'You'll think me right slow, Sheriff, but who is this man we're talking about here?'

'Ah, don't fox with me, Mr Lowry. Your pa's sharp as a lancet and I've an idea his son takes after him. I'm talking about a fellow by the name of Mick Dyson.'

'Wasn't that the man as had his wife murdered?'

'Oh, you're too clever for me, Mr Lowry, too clever by half! Yes, that's the fellow.'

Tom Lowry wasn't altogether sure how best to proceed, although he felt that his father's inquiry of Sheriff Carver had presented him with an opportunity to advance his own investigations. He said, 'But I thought that case was all over and settled. Didn't I hear where somebody was sentenced for the murder?'

'Murder? This ain't about the murder. It's a horse of another colour.'

Hoping that his father would forgive him for the deception, Lowry thought that this was too good a chance to miss and that he could perhaps bluff the sheriff into revealing what he knew about Mick Dyson. Taking a deep breath, Tom Lowry said, 'Fact of the matter is, Sheriff, a federal marshal has applied to my father for a warrant in a big case, I can't tell you the details. This Mick Dyson's name was mentioned, but my father wasn't sure the evidence was sound and so he wouldn't issue the warrant. I offered to come down here before my final bar examinations to look around. Seemingly he didn't trust me to handle it properly and so he's contacted you as well.'

'Son of a bitch!' exclaimed Sheriff Carver, adding hastily, 'not meaning to refer to your pa, you understand. Mind you, your father's a regular devil. No offence meant.'

'None taken, I do assure you.'

'Always seems to know what's going on, anywhere in the country.'

'You should have tried growing up with him,' said Tom Lowry, 'and attempting to conceal an illicit visit to the cookie jar.'

Sheriff Carver laughed at that and Lowry wondered if this would lighten the mood enough for him to work out what Carver's interest was in Mick Dyson. The sheriff said, 'Marshal's after Dyson, is that how the land lies? Damned if he'll get him. Dyson's mine. I've been on his track long enough.'

'I don't know a whole lot about this, Sheriff. My father just wanted me to ask a few questions. I gather it's an important business, though, and that if he grants this warrant, then a bunch of marshals will be arriving here to arrest Dyson.'

'Well then, it's time to lay things down. Here's my side o' the case. Mick Dyson's been in and around this town for years now. First one thing, then another.

One time, I thought he was riding with a bunch of road agents, but then he looked to have married and settled down on a farm, out by Innocence. Lately, though, he's thrown in with some men here and from all I'm able to collect, they're coining. Maybe farming doesn't pay well enough, I wouldn't know about that. You're an attorney, so you know that's a federal matter, forging currency. I guess the Treasury might be on their tail for it. But I want to be the one who nails him. It don't matter why, but it's important for me that it's me as makes the arrest and not some Treasury agent or federal marshal, see?'

At odd times over the last few years, while he had been studying at law school, Tom Lowry had doubted his ability to become a competent attorney. He felt that he lacked the cunning to draw unwilling admissions from hostile witnesses in court or to engage in the verbal gymnastics that were so necessary in the courtroom. This little exchange, though, had given him to hope that he had been wrong. His father had sent a simple inquiry about this business to the sheriff and he, Tom Lowry, had managed to manipulate the man into giving him chapter and verse of his private business; telling him all manner of things that he might not have wished to let out. Maybe he would make it as an attorney yet!

'You want that I should get my father to hold off for a couple of days on granting the warrant?' asked Lowry, in apparent amazement. 'Sheriff, you're asking me to compound a felony!'

'It can't matter overmuch to you. Maybe we could do each other a favour. You're going to be a practising attorney soon, I'm sure you know that it's worth building up good will among peace officers.'

'That's true. Level with me; when are you planning to take Dyson and his associates?'

'Three days from now. I need to get together some men I can trust and then we're going to hit them all at the same time.'

'All right, Sheriff Carver. You got a deal. I'll stall my father and get him to hold off for three days. But don't you forget the favour.'

In his own mind, Will Bennett was more or less certain now that it had been Mick Dyson himself who had killed his own wife; shocking as the idea was. The man must then have set out quite deliberately and cold-bloodedly to pin the blame on somebody else. It struck Bennett that this was probably why Dyson had engaged him in the first place, to play the role of patsy in his wicked scheme.

Presumably, he already had some kind of love affair going with the woman running the hardware store right here in Dallas. Was that the motive for murdering his wife? Perhaps that would never be known for certain. Will Bennett looked up at the clock hanging above Main Street. It was almost time for him to go down to the railroad depot and meet Tom Lowry. He wondered what Lowry might have uncovered during his investigations in Innocence.

111

Since seeing Dyson and finding out that he was courting some woman so soon after the death of his poor wife, Will Bennett's priorities had shifted slightly. When first he had arrived back in Dallas, his only aim was to clear his name and ensure that people knew he was no murderer. Now, having worked out that Mick Dyson might have been responsible both for the murder and also for setting him up to take the blame, Bennett was beginning to think that obtaining justice for his own self might not be sufficient. What about that poor dead woman lying in her grave? Didn't she deserve justice as well? Who would speak for her?

At the depot, Lowry and Bennett met and then walked off to confer. Both men were taken aback by what the other had to report and, put together, their information left neither in any doubt that Mick Dyson was a nasty piece of work who had almost certainly killed his wife.

'That's the hell of a thing,' said Will Bennett, when they had finished exchanging notes. 'From what I can make out, it could be that Dyson only married his wife for her money or property or whatever. What a cur!'

'That's as maybe. More to the point for us is that in a few days' time, Sheriff Carver will be taking him into custody on quite a different matter. If we don't act soon, I don't see that you're ever going to be able to clear your name. He's hardly going to admit to murder once he's being held on a charge of forgery.'

'That means that I must work fast,' said Bennett imperturbably. 'Will you help me a little more or are you bound for home now?'

'Don't be crazy, man. Of course I'll carry on helping you.'

'This is what I purpose . . .' began Will Bennett.

Mick Dyson was convinced that something bad was waiting for him if he didn't move pretty sharpish. He had been hoping to stay in Dallas more or less permanently now that he had sold the farm. He was genuinely fond of Hattie Charlton and had half hoped to settle down with her here; at least after a decent interval had elapsed since the death of his first wife. Now, though, Dyson didn't think that that project was on the cards after all, which was a shame.

Even before his marriage to Amelia, Dyson had been in the habit of making what he was pleased to call 'business trips' to Dallas. When talking to the folk in Innocence, he was vague as to the nature of the business which necessitated these trips and even after he was living with Amelia, he would vanish for anything from a day to a fortnight, handling his mysterious business. It was because his wife had been growing increasingly troublesome about his regular absences from home that he had decided that it was time to be rid of her. Every time in the last year that he had returned from Dallas, Amelia claimed to find evidence of his infidelity; red hairs on his clothing, another woman's scent and suchlike. It had become a positive nuisance.

Dyson had experienced no moral scruples about disposing of his wife. He had never loved her or any foolishness of that sort. It was simply that she was a good-looking woman with a substantial property in her own name. Having made the decision that his wife should go, it was typical of the sort of man that Mick Dyson was that he try to glean as much advantage from Amelia's death as was humanly possible.

Three months before he murdered his wife, Dyson insured her life with two different companies in Dallas; each policy being for five thousand dollars and with double indemnity clauses which would, in the case of accidental death or homicide, bring in a total of twenty thousand dollars. The premiums had been crippling, but he knew that in a case of this sort, nothing could be hurried. When it was a case of murder, the insurance companies would be unlikely to pay out unless somebody other than the beneficiary was actually convicted of the crime.

Seeing Will Bennett riding along the highway that day had been like the answer to a man's prayers. He was a loner and an outsider. Dyson had invited him to share a meal with them and then had come that stupendous stroke of good fortune, when Bennett had revealed his infirmity. It was as though this sap had been tailor-made for the part of the killer.

The murder itself went as smooth as silk. When he returned that night, Amelia told him that the new hired man had retired to the barn with one of his headaches. It was a sure bet that Bennett would be out for a few hours and then, according to what he had already told them, he would have little or no memory of what had chanced for the previous three or four hours. He had forced himself violently upon his wife and then stabbed her repeatedly and smeared some blood on the slumbering drifter snoring torturously in the barn. A sprinkling of whiskey and the stage was set.

As soon as the jury brought him in guilty and sentence of death was passed, Mick Dyson had gone straight off to the insurance companies and claimed on the policies on his late wife's life. Neither of the companies were overly enthusiastic about paying out, that was for sure, but there was little enough they could do about it. The court had ruled that Amelia Dyson had died violently at the hands of somebody other than the beneficiary named on the policies and they were accordingly liable to pay out ten thousand dollars on each of them. Dyson hadn't wanted anything other than cash money and there had been a little dickering about that at first. Now, it was all arranged. Not tomorrow, but the next day, he would be able to collect what he thought of as his 'winnings' and when once that money was in his possession, he was heading west; as far as ever he could get from Texas.

How he knew that he was under observation, Dyson couldn't have said. He was pretty sure that it was nothing to do with the death of his wife, because that was all finished with. It had given him something of a shock to hear that Will Bennett had escaped en route to Kansas, but he hadn't been heard of since, so most likely that didn't signify. No, this had reference to the coining operation that he and one or two other like-minded individuals had going in a farmhouse a little out of town.

For years now, Dyson had had various little operations going in Dallas. This latest, which he had organized seven months previously, was one of the easiest and most profitable in which he had been involved. Coining was a straightforward enough enterprise; always provided, of course, that you knew what you were about. He and three other men were turning out fair to middling imitations of silver dollars by means of casting in moulds. The finished products of this operation were passable, as long as they were not scrutinized too closely. They were made from a pewter alloy containing no lead, something along the lines of Britannia Metal. The chief constituent was tin, with a small quantity of antimony and a little copper added for hardness. Due to the high melting point of the metals used, a furnace was necessary and so the men had taken a lease on a remote house, with no nearby neighbours who might inquire into what was causing the constant, foul-smelling smoke and fumes that were produced.

None of the four men involved in this game ever passed these coins themselves. Instead, they sold them at half their face value to others. Since each coin cost only a cent or two to produce and were

being sold for fifty cents each, the profits were con-
siderable.

Somehow, somebody had screwed up. Mick Dyson
knew that he was being followed. Not all the time,
but often enough to convince him that his move-
ments were of interest to somebody. Was it the law or
some gang that had it in mind to move in on Dyson's
racket? He didn't know and nor did he particularly
care. It was enough that he was no longer safe in
Dallas. If he stayed much longer then either he
would be arrested or perhaps embroiled in some
deadly fight over the coining operation. Neither
prospect was appetizing for a man who would, in
another forty-eight hours, have twenty thousand
dollars in cash in his pockets. It was time to get out of
Dallas for good.

'What I have in mind,' said Bennett, 'is that I lure
Dyson somewhere so that he and I can talk straight,
man to man. He'll have no need to lie to me about
his wife's death and I'll tax him with it outright.'

'Suppose he turns you in or just shoots you out of
hand?' asked the practical Tom Lowry.

'Well now, that's where you come in,' said Will
Bennett hesitantly.

'Me? Fat lot of good I'd be in a rough house. I'm
not the fighting kind.'

Will Bennett laughed at that. 'No, I didn't mean
that you should fight him. I was thinking more that
you might hear if he confesses and then you could

make a statement, saying what he said. That would have some weight in a court, wouldn't it?'

'It might. It just might,' said Lowry, thinking that he had underestimated the quiet, shy man's intelligence. 'Mind, there'd be a big risk for you. He might want to silence you for good and all.'

'That's a chance I'll have to take, I guess.'

CHAPTER 9

When Judge Lowry had written to the sheriff in Dallas, inquiring about one Michael Dyson, he had simply been trying to find out if there were any official misgivings about the verdict which promised to send Will Bennett to the gallows. He was not to know about the coining operation in which Dyson was involved, nor that his son Tom would build an elaborate fantasy around the telegram that Sheriff Carver had received. In fact, the telegram dispatched by Judge Lowry acted to precipitate the subsequent bloody events, which had not been the judge's intention at all.

The first consequence of Judge Lowry's casual inquiry was that Sheriff Carver got it into his head that US Treasury agents were likely to descend upon his town and snatch Mick Dyson and his three fellow forgers, turning the whole affair into a federal case. This was not at all what Carver wanted. He was coming up for re-election shortly and it was in his best interests to have an important triumph like this to his credit. Uncovering and breaking up a gang of forgers would impress the good citizens of Dallas no end.

Another unintended result of that telegram and the talk which Sheriff Carver later had with Judge Lowry's son, was that Carver increased his surveillance of Mick Dyson and his fellows in crime. Dyson, who had already been aware that he was under observation, became spooked by this and determined to speed up his departure from town. It was while he was in a state of almost feverish anxiety and trying as best he could to accelerate the plans for his relocation to California that Dyson arose one morning to find a folded piece of paper lying outside his front door, weighted down with a stone. It said:

> You are in great danger. Everything is known, both about the murder and your present activities. If you would escape with your life, then follow these instructions to the very letter. Two miles from town, out on the road to Sherman, is an old, dilapidated barn. If you arrive there an hour after the sun has set this day, then you will learn something to your advantage.

This mysterious communication was signed, 'A well-wisher'.

The letter left at Dyson's house was largely the

work of Tom Lowry, who, despite the seriousness of the matter in which he was involved, could not help but feel a sense of schoolboy glee at the chance to send such a message. It was straight out of a dime novel or penny dreadful and the young attorney stored up this incident in his memory, conscious that it would one day make a first-class after-dinner story.

The effect that the few lines on that sheet of paper had upon the recipient exceeded all expectations that the authors could possibly have entertained. Mick Dyson was terrified out of his senses by the discovery that somebody apparently knew that he and not the hired man had killed his wife. Being taken for coining would have been bad enough, and the letter hinted that this too was known about, but the other was a hanging matter. It is no exaggeration to say that Dyson was as frightened as a man could be by learning that somebody in town knew all this about him.

That morning, Mick Dyson made a number of visits around Dallas, all of them of a strictly business nature. These meetings did not all go precisely as he might have wished. His first call was to the attorney who was handling the sale of the farm near Innocence. A buyer had been found, but the process would take something over a month before the money was ready to draw on. This was far too long for comfort and when he left Dallas, Dyson didn't want to provide anybody with a forwarding address and so, regretfully, he mentally wrote off the farm. Naturally, he said nothing of this to the attorney, merely assuring him that he would keep in regular touch.

The next visit of the day was more pleasant. One of the insurance companies was pleased to tell Mr Dyson that the ten thousand dollars was ready and waiting for him at the First National Bank of Texas and he could collect his money whenever he was minded to do so. This was heartening and went some way towards ameliorating the blow which he received at the next office to which he went. This company told Dyson that an objection had been raised to paying out on the policy issued against the life of the late Mrs Amelia Dyer and that they would notify him within a week just what the nature of that objection might be.

By the time he returned to the house he was renting, at around midday, Dyson was feeling moderately satisfied with the way things had gone that morning. He had not been so sanguine as to expect that all his cards would come up aces and the news that he was now worth ten thousand dollars was not at all a bad outcome. It was a shame about the other policy and a nuisance about the farm, but then things never go all the way that you might hope. Ten thousand dollars was surely enough to set him up quite comfortably in Sacramento.

There were, it seemed from where Mick Dyson found himself that day, only two things to accomplish before he dug up and headed west. One of these was to withdraw the whole of the ten thousand dollars owing to him by the insurance company, in cash, and the other was to kill whoever it was who had written that cryptic message that he had found on his porch that morning. So it was that after a light meal, Dyson cleaned and loaded his pistol and then went down to the bank and collected the large sum of money waiting for him there.

Jed Carver, Sheriff of Dallas, now had everything in place for his coup. He would really have preferred to wait another week or two, until the case was at what he regarded as the correct stage for him to act, but it had turned into a race against time. With, as he supposed, federal agents in Kansas trying to obtain a warrant for one of his suspects and who knew what others interested in the affair, he needed to get those men into his own custody as soon as was humanly possible. Even if he was compelled to allow their extradition to another state at some later date, the publicity of having caught them would be all in his own name. Tomorrow morning at ten, he and his men would swoop and every one of those fellows would be behind bars within an hour at the outside.

As he rode along the Sherman Road, heading north out of Dallas, Mick Dyson turned over in his mind that peculiar letter which suggested the time and place of the meeting which he was about to attend. It was evidently someone who knew that he had murdered his wife, but that being so, why had this person not gone to the sheriff with such information? For Dyson, crooked to the core as he was, there could be but one explanation for this. Obviously, this was an attempt to blackmail him and deprive him of the money which he had made from his wife's death. Was it some clerk in the insurance company? That was certainly possible. Well, this individual would learn tonight that Michael Dyson was not a man to trifle or be trifled with. He had already committed one murder and the second time you do anything is always a deal easier than the first. From all that he could collect, somebody would be waiting for him in that barn, a man who was able to place the noose around Dyson's neck, if he so chose. There never was any point in paying off a blackmailer, because they would always come back for more. Far better to take a strong line right from the very start.

The sun had set and the landscape was fading into shades of sepia as Dyson reined in near the old barn. He dismounted and tethered his horse to a tree stump. Then, he drew his pistol, cocking it with his thumb as he did so. The person hiding in that barn thought that he could get one over on Michael Dyson, did he? He would learn the error of his ways before he died.

Dyson wasn't worried about the possibility of walking into an ambush. Having decided that this was almost certainly a case of blackmail, he knew that no blackmailer in his senses shares his information with others. No, there would be only one single man in that barn and his intention would be to put the bite on Dyson and see how much he could screw him for. It was almost twilight and the interior of the barn looked dark and uninviting. Still, he had a thirty-six Colt in his hand, loaded and cocked. He would be able to draw down on the waiting man and shoot him before the other had a chance to draw himself. Still, Dyson's strategy was predicated on the assumption that he was dealing with a blackmailer. There never was a victim of blackmail murdered by the man who is blackmailing him. That would be a case of killing the goose that laid the golden egg!

It took a second for Mick Dyson's eyes to adjust to the stygian darkness of the barn. He looked round, unable at first to see anything much. There were various pieces of rusty farm machinery standing in the shadows, as well as lengths of timber and other oddments including, as Dyson saw when once his eyes became accustomed to the gloom, a man sitting on the floor with a pistol in his hand; a pistol which was pointing straight at Mick Dyson's face.

'Whoa there,' said Dyson, not lowering his own gun, but neither making any aggressive move, 'what's to do? Looks to me like we both of us each got the other covered. You want that we should lower our pieces?'

'No,' said the man seated in the shadows, 'I don't believe that I do.'

Something about the man's voice sounded familiar to Dyson, although it took him a little while to recollect the person to whom it belonged. When he did so, a cold chill ran up his spine and he knew that death had entered that dark barn and was even now standing at his side, ready to clap its hand upon his shoulder. For several seconds, the two men remained frozen, the one sitting and the other standing, both pointing their guns at each other.

It was Will Bennett who broke the tense and uncomfortable silence, saying, 'You mind who I am, Dyson?'

'Yes, I know you. Heard you'd escaped, but I didn't think you'd be such a damned fool as to come back here.'

'Did you not?' asked Bennett, 'you thought I'd run?'

'So what did you come back for?'

'You're a mangy cur, Dyson. You killed your own wife and then did your damnedest to see me hanged for your crime. Your conscience never trouble you 'bout any of that?'

'You don't know how I was placed. It's easy to judge a man when you don't know what he's been up against.'

'There's nothing can excuse the murder of a woman. Nothing.'

Dyson said nothing for a space as they maintained their position of each keeping the other covered. Then he said, 'Don't be sore. You were such a godsend to me, I'd o' been a fool not to take advantage. When you told us that first night about that affliction of yours, why I nearly jumped for joy.'

'You stand there and tell me so?' asked Bennett, his voice level and unemotional.

'It was nothing personal, man. I had my tail in a crack and you chanced along. It was business.'

'Some business,' said Will Bennett contemptuously. 'What happened on the night of the murder? Your wife tell you when you got home from Dallas that I'd been taken with one of my turns?'

'Something like that. I knew I'd never have a better opportunity.'

'So you killed her and laid the blame at my door. Splashed some whiskey and blood on me as I slept and then made out it was me all along.'

'Hell, what d'you want me to say? That I'm sorry? Such things happen. Why d'you drag me all the way out here? You already know what happened.'

'I wanted it from your own lips, Dyson, that's all.'

'Now you got it. What then, that's all? You're still wanted, you know. Don't think o' showing yourself in town or you'll be taken right back to prison.'

There was something about the behaviour and overall attitude of Will Bennett that puzzled Mick Dyson. He could not quite put his finger on it, but he was dissatisfied and a mite uneasy. He'd be gone the next day, so it didn't really matter what this sap thought he knew. It would have eased his mind greatly to make an end to Bennett there and then, but Dyson was sharp enough to know that even if he just pulled the trigger, then there was every prospect that this would cause Bennett to do the same and then he'd feel pretty silly. This hulking oaf was harmless enough and could be forgotten about in another twenty-four hours. Very slowly, and without bidding the other man farewell, Dyson backed out of the barn and then walked swiftly to his horse, taking frequent looks over his shoulder to see if he was being pursued.

If it hadn't been for the fact that Mick Dyson had convinced himself beforehand that he was about to encounter a lone blackmailer, then he might at some point have wondered if he and Bennett were alone in that barn. They had not been. The entire time that he had been talking with Bennett, a man up in the hayloft and out of sight, had a gun trained on him. Tom Lowry did not know if he would be able to squeeze the trigger if it came down to it, nor whether, having done so, he would be likely to hit anybody. Like as not, Lowry thought after he and Bennett once again had the barn to themselves, he would have ended up putting a bullet through Will Bennett, rather than his intended target!

Once the two men heard the hoof beats fading into the distance, Tom Lowry climbed down the ladder to rejoin his companion. Bennett said, 'You got any doubts about me, now?'

'I never had any to begin with,' said Lowry truthfully. 'The main thing is that I have actually heard Michael Dyson admit to murder and I can swear out an affidavit to that effect. I can see us clearing your name in next to no time.'

'It's not enough.'

'What do you mean, it's not enough? Isn't that what you want?'

Bennett gave a short laugh. 'Of course it's what I want. But there's something more. I want to see Mick Dyson brought to account for that murder. I want to be sure he answers for it.'

Something in Will Bennett's tone of voice told Lowry that this determination to see the guilty punished was more than some personal grudge on Bennett's part. The man really was devoted to justice in a way that he, Tom Lowry, was not. For him, even though he had trained as an attorney and was hoping one day to be a judge like his father, the law was an elaborate and sophisticated game, whose rules he had been carefully learning for the last few years. His studies had had little or nothing to do with the abstract idea of justice, which mattered so very much to Bennett. Not for the first time, Lowry thought that there might be a good deal more to this quiet, unassuming fellow than met the eye. As they went to fetch their horses, which had been left a couple of fields away to avoid giving Dyson cause to suspect that there might be more than one person waiting in the barn, Lowry said, 'You never think to be something in the legal line? Study law, maybe work for a sheriff's office or something?'

'Oh, I ain't cut out for that kind of thing.'

*

He was not being followed or watched the whole time, of that Dyson was sure. Just then and when, at odd times. That was fine, because he would be vanishing the next day. He had booked his ticket and would be shaking the dust of Dallas from his feet, once for all. Before that, though, he had only one last bit of work and that would be to ride out to the lonely farmhouse where the three men with whom he had set up the coining operation lived. He owed it to them at least to bid goodbye. Sentiment alone did not motivate this final visit; there was something in the region of five hundred dollars owing to him and since he would not apparently be getting anything for the sale of the farm, nor from one of the insurance companies, it seemed crazy not to collect a tidy sum of cash money which was just waiting there for him. He was not so rich that he could afford to let five hundred dollars slip through his fingers.

As Mick Dyson was preparing for a good long sleep, Tom Lowry and Will Bennett were sitting and chatting about their next course of action. Lowry knew perfectly well that Sheriff Carver was likely to take Dyson into custody soon over the forging of currency. That was fine; at least there would then be no possibility of the fellow simply disappearing. It was a matter of some urgency, though, for Lowry to swear out an affidavit, setting out precisely what he had heard Dyson admitting to. Combined with the information he had picked up in the town of Innocence, Lowry was convinced that there was sufficient evidence to have the verdict of the court in the matter of the State of Texas versus William Bennett overturned and rendered null and void. That would mean that Will Bennett was no longer legally regarded as a murderer and the way would be open to charge Dyson with his wife's murder.

'You see what this means?' Lowry asked his companion, 'you'd be free as the wind and no taint whatever attached to your name.'

'It's right good of you to take all this trouble for me,' said Will Bennett, 'I owe you and your father a deal.'

'Don't talk such nonsense. You could have cut and run after that stage was held up, but you wouldn't abandon my mother and sister. What I'm doing is nothing set against that. Nothing at all. You put your very life in danger for them. All I'm doing is spending a little time on practical legal work before sitting my final examinations.'

'I'm not feeling too perky this evening,' announced Bennett abruptly, 'I've a headache coming on. I'd best retire early, but before I do, I want your advice.'

'Fire away.'

'It's about your sister,' began Bennett and coloured slightly in embarrassment. 'She's kind o' . . . well, sweet on me. So I think, anyways.'

'Sure, I noticed it too. What of it?'

'I said I'd write her. I want you to help me with the

letter. I want to write it tonight.'

Tom Lowry felt inclined to burst out laughing at this request. The very idea of it; a man helping write a letter to his sister from somebody to whom she had taken a fancy. He'd never heard the like! He said quietly, 'What do you want to say to her, Will?'

'She's only a kid. I like her very much, but Lord, after all that I've seen and done in my life and her just fresh out of school! Maybe there ain't more than six or seven years' difference in our ages, but she's an innocent child compared with me. But I don't want to shame her by sayin' that exactly. I want you to help me tell her that I like her very much, but our lives are so different that it would be madness to think we could get close like . . . like that. You think you can help me say all that?'

Not for the first time, Lowry was struck by the extraordinary delicacy shown by this ill-educated wanderer. He might be rough and ready, but Will Bennett had the heart and soul of a natural-born gentleman, for all of that. 'I'll lend you a hand, though I think that you'd probably manage well enough without my assistance. You have a rare talent for divining what's fitting and right.'

'I'm not in that mould. I just know that your sister is an innocent. It would be a sin to mar that, but I figure a girl like her might be put out to be told that she's too young and innocent for the likes of me.'

'You're right there. She thinks herself no end of a

132

woman of the world. She'd never forgive you. Wait while I fetch paper and pen and we'll see what we can do between the two of us.'

CHAPTER 10

Sheriff Carver had recruited a substantial body of men to help him in the raid on the farmhouse where he was sure that the coiners had their lair. He intended to hit the farm and also the rented house in town where Mick Dyson resided simultaneously, at ten in the morning. Even now, Carver was tormented by the fear that he might be too late and that he would arrive at that remote property five miles from town, only to find a bunch of federal marshals and Treasury agents already in control of the place. He would have struck earlier, but it had been no easy task to put together such a large posse, every member of which could be trusted not to shoot his mouth off about the forthcoming raid while in his cups.

The men assembled at eight that morning outside the sheriff's office. They were all mounted and armed to the teeth, although Sheriff Carver had told them that he didn't anticipate much trouble from these fellows and hoped that they would come quietly. At about the same time that the first men began to arrive at the sheriff's office, Mick Dyson was leaving his house with a valise containing a change of clothes, his shaving tackle and ten thousand dollars in high denomination bills. He aimed to ride north to Sherman, picking up the stage there and then making his way west once he was in Kansas. Even now, Dyson was not fully determined to ride out first to the farm in order to collect the money which was owing to him. What finally decided him was the fact that he had, as he saw it, been cheated out of the other ten thousand dollars by the damned insurance office. That still rankled, for he had been counting on that money. So, in the end, he thought that he might just as well pick up five hundred dollars, which was his, and was waiting for him out at the farmhouse where the other three were living.

There were enough people about on the streets of Dallas at that time of day for Dyson not to be able to scrutinize closely every passing rider or pedestrian. Indeed, such attention to those around him would have been counter-productive, for Mick Dyson's chief aim that day was to appear as casual and unguarded as any other honest citizen going about his business. He went down to where his horse was being kept at livery, raising his hat to people he recognized and smiling cheerfully and bidding a good morning to those he did not. In short, there could scarcely have been a more natural, good-natured and inoffensive man in the whole of Dallas that morning. Certainly, Dyson did not peer around nervously to see if he was being followed; that would have given altogether the wrong impression for the character which he had adopted.

Will Bennett had gone immediately to bed after Lowry had helped him compose a suitable letter to Bella. His headache was raging now and he knew that if he did not get into bed, he ran the risk of collapsing in a dead faint, and that would not do.

Although they had only known each other for a matter of days, Bennett knew instinctively that he could trust the other man implicitly. Tom Lowry was one of those men who, when once they had given their word, would follow it through to the bitter end, come hell or high water. He had not the least apprehension that Lowry would neglect the part he had promised to play in clearing Will's name. No, that aspect of things could safely be left in other hands now and he could concentrate upon the more important question of calling Dyson to account for his actions.

That Bennett's own name would be restored and the taint of murder removed from it, Bennett himself was confident. That the real murderer would face justice, he was less sure. Having seen how readily the law had convicted an innocent man and very nearly consigned him to the gallows for a crime in which he had had no part, it was hardly surprising that Will

Bennett's faith in due, judicial process was a little shaky. Better by far, he thought, to do things his own way and make sure of the job.

Of one thing, Will Bennett was sure. It would not do at all to involve Lowry in this day's work. Tom Lowry had a bright future ahead of him as an attorney and probably one day, a judge like his father. The last thing he needed was to be roped into some illegal activity before he had even properly qualified. Bennett guessed that his friend would insist upon helping out if told what the plan was, and so it seemed better to Will Bennett just to slip out of the house early and leave Lowry sleeping.

From half past five that morning, the house that Mick Dyson had rented was under observation from a distance by a quiet-looking young man on horseback. When the door opened at eight, Bennett withdrew a little into the shadows and then followed on to see where Dyson was heading. It came as no surprise when he saw the man entering the livery stables on the edge of town. There were other riders about and so as long as he kept a good long way behind Dyson, there was no earthly reason why he should spook his quarry.

All in all, Mick Dyson was now feeling absolutely on top of the world. The encounter yesterday with the man he'd set up to take the blame for Amelia's death had been a little unnerving at the time, but he couldn't see where it was likely to cause him any problems. Let Bennett show his face near the sheriff's office and try to blame somebody else for the murder, and he would be arrested at once and carted off to the federal penitentiary. Even if the case were to be reopened, then Dyson would be long gone. So it was that he trotted along the road as free as a bird, his mind full of the wonderful things that he would be able to do in Sacramento with ten thousand dollars in his pocket.

The three men who had been doing much of the hard and unpleasant work which coining entails, were not yet awake as Dyson rode up to the farmhouse. These men, from whom Sheriff Carver was not expecting any real trouble, were actually as deadly as angry rattlers. It had been Dyson who had set up the casts, imported the little furnace and arranged for the supplies of tin, antimony and copper. None of the three men living in that house would have been capable of devising a scheme of that sort.

Jake Parker, 'Spurs' Wilson and Jim Bacon had all known each other for some time before they had met up with Dyson. Their usual line of work was more hit and run attacks on lonely farms or robbing travellers in out-of-the-way places. Dyson had persuaded them that there was a sight more money and a lot less risk in making snide currency than there was in doing hold-ups. With games like that, there was always a very real possibility that some concerned citizens would band together into an informal court and string men up from a tree after the most cursory of trials. Somehow, forging silver dollars didn't arouse the same anger in ordinary folk, who were content to let the regular law enforcement authorities tackle cases of forgery in their own good time.

By and large, the men who lived in the old house had found Dyson to be perfectly right and although keeping the furnace going was an arduous and irksome business, especially in this warm weather, on the whole the work was easier than riding down stagecoaches or laying siege to some homestead. All good things come to an end, though, and the three of them knew that this part of the country must by now be about flooded with their tin coins. Mick Dyson had intimated as much to them a few days back and so they had been gradually winding down operations here and packing the materials up with a view to shifting across the state line.

Forging coins is not a very taxing piece of work. Essentially, it entails making a mould, using a real coin, from fine plaster of Paris and then melting together the tin, copper and antimony and pouring it into the mould. Once you have made your moulds and have a supply of materials, it is simple enough to turn out hundreds of coins each day. True, it is hot and dirty work, but the rewards are exceedingly high.

When Dyson walked through the door and hollered out for the others, Jake Parker stirred and called down, 'That you, Mick? Whyn't you get the stove going and set a pot of coffee on it. We'll be down directly.'

Grumbling to himself about being treated like a damned skivvy, Dyson nevertheless went into the kitchen and got the fire going. It lacked a few minutes to nine before the three occupants of the house deigned to wander down the stairs to greet him blearily. They had been up to a late hour the previous night, drinking and gaming.

'So what's the news, Mick me fellow?' inquired Wilson. 'Anything happening in town as we should know of?'

'To put the case in a nutshell,' said Dyson, 'it's time to move on. I've been watched at odd times lately. Not all the time and not always by the same person, but somebody's taking an interest in my affairs. Since this is the only iron I got in the fire right now, you can bet it's on account of this business.'

'Ah, shit,' said Wilson irritably, 'that's a damned shame. Somebody talked, you think?'

'I wouldn't o' thought so. More that too many of our little pieces of artwork have been turning up in Dallas and that cowson sheriff has marked me as somebody who ain't averse to making a buck by crooked means. That's nothing to the purpose. It simply means we got to dig up and leave.'

The four of them had poured coffee and Mick Dyson was on the point of broaching the small matter of the five hundred dollars of his that he would like to have this very morning, when there came an unexpected and alarming development. This took the form of a large stone hurled through

140

the window of the kitchen in which they were sitting and taking their ease. There were various expressions of anger and amazement, along the lines of, 'Shit!', 'Son of a bitch!' and 'What the hell?' Then, before they had a chance to figure out the play, a shout from outside the house claimed their undivided attention.

'You men in there,' yelled Sheriff Carver from a safe position behind a stone wall at the back of the property, 'I strongly recommend that you all come out with your hands held as high as you like!'

This advice was not at all to the liking of the men in the kitchen and, abandoning their coffee, three of them ran up the stairs to where they had left their weapons. Only Mick Dyson remained in the kitchen, moving to the wall by the window and peering cautiously out and trying to gauge how many men were out there. He cursed his greed and cupidity. If only he'd written off those five hundred dollars! As the men came clattering down the stairs, muttering and swearing, Dyson made his own plans. He owed these fellows nothing at all. They had joined together to make money and were not bound to each other by kinship or even affection. Their association was strictly business.

From all that he was able to gather from looking out the window, Dyson did not believe that the house was actually surrounded. There looked to be a half dozen men, poorly concealed behind the trees and bushes which stretched away into the fields. They looked to him to be a fairly compact group and although he would need to check by going to the front of the house, he didn't believe that there were any more than those six, maybe seven, men out there. When the others had joined him in the kitchen, taking care to keep clear of the window, Dyson said, 'I'm going to take a look out front and see how many of those bastards are out there.'

Scanning the area in front of the farmhouse confirmed what Dyson had suspected, that Sheriff Carver and his men were all to be found in the area behind the house. He did not have enough men to surround the place. Although Dyson wasn't to know this, Carver had screwed up badly. In the first place, instead of the twelve men he had hired for his posse, only nine had turned up that morning. Rather than put off the raid, Sheriff Carver had chosen to go ahead with his plans. The fear that he would be beaten to the prize of catching the gang of coiners was to prove the sheriff's undoing; in his hurry to accomplish the mission that day, he'd set out with fewer men than would be necessary.

Carver had decided in his own mind that coiners and bandits were two mutually exclusive classes of criminal. Had he been going up against a bunch of road agents or train robbers, he would not have dreamed of fetching up at that house with just six companions. He had got it into his head somehow that men engaged in forging currency would not be particularly dangerous and would be likely to come

142

along quietly. All of which accounted for the fact that he had sent three men off to Mick Dyson's house to bring that individual in and had set off himself with six men to arrest those he believed to be holed up in the old Manson place.

Will Bennett had tailed Dyson out to the isolated farmhouse, never getting closer than a mile to the man he was following. Bennett found a stand of trees near the house and simply sat there on his horse watching to see what Dyson would do and where he would go after entering the house. One thing that Will Bennett had was patience. It might have been thought that a fellow in his situation would have been as jittery as a scalded cat, but if so, there was no sign of it on the outside. He just sat placidly, waiting to see what would happen next.

A short while after Dyson had gone into the farmhouse, seven riders had approached the place circuitously from the north and Bennett had observed them to dismount and then creep up to the outbuildings without, presumably, being seen from the windows. 'This,' he said quietly, 'is going to be interesting!'

Inside the farmhouse, there had been some brief discussion about what to do. Significantly, the possibility of surrender had not been mentioned by any of the four men. Dyson knew that his perfect plan for murdering his wife had begun to unravel and that with

Will Bennett on the loose, it was altogether possible that Amelia's death would eventually be laid at his door. He for one did not propose to be taken tamely into custody with the prospect of ending up on the gallows. The other three were wanted across three states for various crimes and misdemeanours. Some of these were hanging matters and they too preferred to fight it out, and if that meant the chance of a clean death from a bullet, then so be it.

It was at this critical juncture that Sheriff Jed Carver made the most serious mistake of his whole life. It also happened to be the last mistake he ever made. Unsure after those few minutes' delay in hearing any reply from the men inside the house, Carver thought that because he had been crouching down when he called upon them to come out with their hands up, perhaps his voice had been too muted to be audible within the house. Accordingly, he stood up, filled his lungs with air and then bellowed at the top of his voice, 'Come out with your hands up and there'll be no need for shooting.' Whereupon 'Spurs' Wilson, seeing a clear shot to be had, opened fire, sending a ball straight through Carver's breast.

The sheriff fell to the ground, quite plainly with a mortal wound. The six men near to him, who had only agreed to come along for the fee paid for being part of a posse, were horror-struck. Their dismay was less at the death of a man of whom none were especially fond, but more because they knew that instead of the routine arrests of a fairly harmless crew of forgers, which Sheriff Carver had told them to expect, they were now faced with the risk of death. Hardly had this notion had time to formulate in the minds of the six men crouched behind walls and trees, than a positive hail of fire erupted from the windows of the farmhouse. They could do little, other than to return fire as best they were able. This was starting to look like the hardest five dollars that any of them had ever earned in the whole course of their lives.

The mood inside the Manson place was high. There were four of them and no more than a half dozen outside. Judging by past experience, those half dozen were most likely men who had only signed up for the cash. First off was where they wouldn't be wanting to hazard their lives for five or ten dollars and next was that they were probably not used to exchanging shots like this with determined and ruthless men. This proved to be the case, because the men outside made no real effort to lean from cover to take accurate shots. Their strategy was rather to throw as much lead at the house as they could and hope for the best.

'Hoo boy,' cried Jim Bacon, exhilarated more than alarmed by the number of shots being sent towards the house. 'Those whores' sons don't know shit about work like this.'

'Tell ye what,' said Wilson, 'what say one of us goes up to the attic? There's a little round window up there as would make a perfect sniper's nest. Man up there with a rifle could spot those men and take 'em out one by one.'

'I'll go,' said Bacon. 'I done enough shooting like that in the war.'

A few minutes later, the men downstairs knew that Jim Bacon was as good as his word. There were cracks at irregular intervals as he waited for good targets to present themselves.

Dyson was now ready to leave, but felt instinctively that it would be seen as cowardly were he to run out at the height of the battle. Not that he cared over-much what these men thought of him; it was more that their disapproval might take a very practical form. If they saw him trying to desert them and save his own skin, it was entirely possible that they might shoot him in the back as he left. While he was wrestling with this problem, there came reinforcements for the men besieging the farmhouse.

After realizing that Michael Dyson was not to be found at the address the sheriff had given them, the other three members of the posse had thought it only fair to join the others up at the old Manson place. These three men were cut from a different piece of cloth from the six who had accompanied Sheriff Carver. All had been in Special Forces during the war and had been highly decorated as a consequence. They tended in ordinary life to stick together as a group and so when Carver had asked for three men to go and pick up Dyson, it was logical for the three of them to go. When they arrived at the farmhouse and saw the shambles into which the situation was descending, their professional pride caused them to take charge and see if they could deal with the men inside in a more scientific way.

As the three men came jinking, crouching low as they ran, across the field which lay beyond the pigpens and stone walls at back of the Manson farmhouse, one remarked, 'This is no damned good. See that fellow up top of the house?'

They threw themselves behind a wall and then another said, 'Yeah, they set a man up there to pick us off one by one.'

'Two can play at that game. You fellows keep their sniper busy while I make a break for that barn over yonder. I'm reckoning as there'll be a hayloft there.' He unslung the rifle from his back and then, grasping it tightly, bolted off towards the barn while his two companions concentrated their fire at the round window in the attic. By the time they had stopped and Jim Bacon peeped cautiously out again, the third man was climbing the ladder to the hay loft.

Once he was comfortably ensconced among the bales, Dave Stark wriggled over to the side of the barn that faced the house. Between two of the rough planks of which the wall was formed was a large space; maybe a couple of inches wide. Stark lay on the boards and trained his rifle on the round window at the top of the old farmhouse. He could see a white blob; the face of the man who had chosen that spot as his eyrie. Squinting along the barrel, Stark took a breath, held it, steadied his weapon and then, very gently, squeezed the trigger. Just before he did so, an incongruous smile came unbidden to his lips. He suddenly recalled how the army instructor had warned the new recruits not to pull the trigger when they were aiming. He had said, 'Imagine it's your sweetheart's tit; don't pull it, squeeze!'

Bacon was feeling mighty pleased with himself. He had definitely accounted for two men since he had taken up his post and that meant that there were only four left to deal with. The odds might be even numerically, but he and his comrades surely had the advantage in real terms. He was conning the area below him for another target when a minie ball took him through his left eye, blowing out the back of his head as it exited.

CHAPTER 11

Dyson and the two men in the kitchen had seen the new arrivals and although nothing had been said, the same thought had crossed the minds of each of them; suppose there are more men fetching up behind us? Are we going to be surrounded?

He was not likely to get a better opportunity than this and so Dyson said, 'You fellows stop here. I'm going to check at the front and see if there's any more of those men coming. I reckon we can cope as it is, but if there's more of them. . . .' He let the sentence trail off. If there were more, then it was unlikely that he and the three others would be able to shoot their way out of the trap, was what he meant. Nobody wishes to pronounce their own death sentence, though, and so he left the conclusion unsaid. Parker and Wilson grunted their acquiescence to the plan and so Dyson made his way out of the kitchen and from there to the front parlour.

There was no sign of anybody at this side of the

house and so Mick Dyson crept quietly into the hall, walked along it to the front door and then simply opened it and walked out of the house. He knew that there was a chance that one of those on the other side of the building might see him leaving, but he didn't think it likely. Why those idiots hadn't positioned themselves all round the house, he was unable to say. Perhaps Carver had thought that they really would all come out with their hands up when he called upon them to do so? If so, then he must have been a bigger fool than Dyson had taken him for and that was saying something!

He had left his horse over a slight rise, some fifty yards from the house. Even when there was no real prospect of danger, Mick Dyson often acted that way, just in case. What a mercy he had done so on this occasion, he thought to himself. Imagine if he'd ridden right up to the door and then turned his mount out into the field behind the house. He wouldn't have cared to try to escape on foot.

Clutched in Dyson's hand was the valise that he had packed, containing a few personal effects and the ten thousand dollars from the insurance company. He wondered what Wilson, Bacon and Parker would have said, had they known. Glancing back, he could see that nobody behind the house had noticed that he had left it. Would the men inside be asking themselves where he'd got to by now, or would they have guessed? The crackle of gunfire told him that his erstwhile business partners were fully occupied in the defence of their redoubt. Most likely, they hadn't even set mind to him.

It was an immense relief for Dyson to get over the rise of ground and then scuttle down, so that he could neither see, nor be seen from the house or the area at back of it. By his reckoning, he was pretty well home and dry now. He had hobbled the horse and it had not moved far; grazing contentedly, not thirty feet from where he had left her. With nothing further to delay him, Mick Dyson swung himself into the saddle, secured the valise behind him and trotted off across country, aiming to strike the Sherman road in another two miles. He felt invincible and could scarcely refrain from whistling a cheery little tune. Of the men he had abandoned to their fate, he gave not a single thought. In this world, it was every man for himself.

By the time that Dyson reached the copse stretching up into a low hill, he was feeling more braced with life than he had been at any time since he'd noticed that he was being followed, a few days back. That was until a lone rider walked his horse out from the trees and blocked Dyson's path. The man had a pistol in his hand and it was pointing directly at Dyson. At first, he thought that this might be another member of Carver's damned posse. Then he looked more closely and saw that it was Will Bennett; the one man in the world more than any other who had good reason to want him dead. Despite the bright sun overhead, Dyson shivered. He tried at first to bluff it out, saying, 'Bennett, I know you're vexed with me, but can we not just let bygones be bygones?'

'You'd call your wife's death a "bygone"?' asked Bennett in a flat and passionless voice which was more chilling than any amount of shouting, bluster or brag would have been.

'Come on, man, I won't trouble you. Just let me carry on my way. I'm in the devil of a hurry.'

Bennett smiled faintly at this. 'Yes, I'll be bound you're in a hurry. Men most often are when the shadow of the noose falls upon them. I know just how that feels.' It was hard to know how to respond to this. Dyson was spared the effort of formulating a coherent answer, though, because Bennett continued, still in that same, expressionless and uninflected voice, 'Get down from your horse. Be sure that your hand stays well away from that gun at your hip.'

Every second that he wasted here with this clown increased the chances of Dyson being caught by the posse over at the house. As he dismounted, Bennett said, 'What's all that shooting I can hear, away over yonder? Friends of yours, maybe? You run out on them?'

This was so close to the truth that Dyson shot a sharp look at the man sitting there at his ease on his horse. It could be, he conceded, that Will Bennett was a sight shrewder than he'd given him credit for being. When he was standing on the ground, Dyson turned and said, 'Well, what now? You hold all the cards, so I'm at your mercy, seemingly.'

Not taking his eyes off Dyson for a fraction of a second, Will Bennett got down from the saddle, taking great care to keep his pistol pointing at the other man as he did so. When he was down, he looked Dyson square in the eye and said, 'I'll give you a chance, which is more than you gave me or your poor dead wife.'

At the word 'chance', Dyson's ears pricked up. Had he been in Bennett's place, he would have mercilessly gunned down the man who had nearly got him hanged, but of course Bennett was a man with a code of honour. All his life, Dyson had found it easier to exploit, do down and generally get one over on such people and for the first time since he had recognized Bennett, he felt a faint hope that he would after all be able to wriggle clear of the coils which were threatening to engulf him. He said casually, 'What have you in mind?'

Will Bennett stood looking at the man he had tracked down and thought what a miserable specimen of humanity he was. He said to Dyson, 'I'm offering you a straight duel, just you and me. You tried to have me killed by the law. Well, now I'm giving you a way to do the job yourself, if you think you're up to it.'

He had thought long and hard about this business and as far as Will Bennett could see, this was the most honourable course of action he could take. There was no doubt that Dyson deserved to die for murdering his wife in such a terrible way. Apart from that, this man had done what he could to see Bennett himself killed by others. That was a personal matter and even if he handed Dyson over to the law and saw him hanged for killing his wife, there would be no satisfaction for Bennett's own grievance. On the other hand, he baulked at simply gunning a man down. He said, 'What do you say?'

'How'd you like to play it?'

'I don't trust you, Dyson. We'll do it my way and if by God I see you cheating or trying to gain an edge, I'll shoot you down like a dog. You understand?'

'Sure,' said Dyson without any rancour at being spoken to in this manner. 'So what will you have?'

'I'm going to cover you while you do it. You take that pistol from your holster with your left hand. Very easy, now. Is it loaded?'

'This one is. I was using another back there which is all out of powder.'

'I don't want to hear about that. Set that weapon down on the ground there.'

Dyson looked up nervously. 'You want me to be at your mercy?'

'What's the matter, Dyson?' said Will Bennett, grim amusement flickering round the corners of his mouth, 'don't you trust me? Just do as I say and set down your pistol.'

When the gun was on the ground, Bennett walked over to it and said, 'You step back a pace or two. This here's what we'll do. I'm going to place my own piece next to yours. They're both single action, so neither of us has an advantage there.' Will Bennett suited the actions to the words and placed his pistol carefully on the parched soil next to Dyson's weapon.

'What now?' asked Dyson.

'Now, we both move twenty paces back from the guns and then one of us counts to three. On the count of three, we see which of us can get to his gun first and kill the other.'

Dyson had heard about duellos of this sort, although he had never yet participated in one. He sized up Bennett and wondered whether he was really as slow as he came across. More to the point, was he quick enough on the uptake to know when an opponent planned a double cross? Dyson said, 'What then, we turn our backs on each other?'

'No, we just walk backwards slowly.'

The two men warily began to shuffle backwards, neither of them taking their eyes off the other. Mick Dyson had taken ten paces when he made his move. He dived forward for his pistol and even as he did so, was aware that Will Bennett had not moved; was just standing there, a look of surprise on his face at such treachery. This at least was the impression Dyson had, very briefly, as his hand went out and closed around the hilt of his pistol. And still, that slow-moving oaf had not moved forward. It was not until Dyson had actually cocked his piece and was raising it to fire, that Will Bennett reached swiftly back to where he had another Colt Navy tucked into the back of his pants. He drew this, cocking it as he did so in one fluid movement and then fired twice at Dyson; one ball taking the man in the wrist holding the gun and the second drilling straight through his chest. As the pistol dropped from his nerveless fingers and he keeled over backwards, crashing to the earth like a dead weight, the last words he heard before he lost consciousness were from Bennett, saying, 'I gave you your chance. But I told you I'd shoot you down if you cheated.'

Standing there, watching Mick Dyson breathe his last, Bennett did not feel that he had behaved badly. Imagine if he had been foolish enough to trust that snake! If Dyson had observed the rules of the contest, then he would have had an excellent chance of laying Bennett in his grave. But there it was; men like that didn't seem able to help themselves somehow and always chose the wrong path, the one which led to destruction. With which melancholy reflection, Will Bennett prepared to leave the scene and head north into the Indian Nations. He had agonized somewhat over what to do about the horse which Tom Lowry had rented for him, but thought that turning the creature loose might lead to its finding its own way back again. So he hoped, but if not, then it couldn't be helped. He would need a horse now and the most just and equitable solution to that problem was standing close by, impassively chewing upon what little dusty grass was to be found near at hand. Mick Dyson would certainly have no further use for his horse. As for the dead man's belongings, well he would have a look at those later.

Before mounting up and riding north, Bennett looked down at the body of the man he had slain and said, 'If ever a fellow had that coming to him, that man was you. Even when given a chance, you couldn't help but see it as weakness in another person. I should say that we are even now.' Then he swung himself into the saddle and trotted off. In a way, he felt a little bad about not bidding a proper farewell to Tom Lowry, but figured that Lowry would understand. Just like him and Mick Dyson, so too was Bennett now square with Lowry; at least, as far as he could make out. He'd saved the lives of Tom's mother and sister and in return, Tom had helped him to clear his name and exact vengeance on Mick Dyson. Things balanced out well enough there.

Nathaniel Gold had told Bennett that there was a place waiting for him if he returned and he had a notion that Gold was a man of his word, somebody who said precisely what he meant. That was where he was going to head first and then, well, who knew? He could depend upon Tom to make sure that everybody knew he was innocent of murder and so he was not going to be a fugitive or aught of that sort, which was a mercy. All in all, things were looking pretty good this day.

As soon as he awoke that morning, later than usual, at about eleven, Tom Lowry knew instinctively that Bennett had gone. He checked Bennett's room, but, just as he had suspected, his things were gone. There was no point haring off after him; Bennett knew best what he was about. The news reached Dallas some time after midday about the shootout with coiners. The bodies of those who had died in the battle were brought back to town and Tom Lowry was glad to see that Will Bennett was not among them.

Lowry was sorry that he would probably never set eyes upon Will Bennett again, but knew too that it was perhaps for the best. There was nothing keeping him now in Dallas and if he wasn't to face the prospect of failing miserably at his bar examinations, then he needed to get back to Burfield and get down to some serious studying. Besides which he would have to deliver Bennett's letter to his sister.

Apart from a little help with spelling and punctuation, the letter that Will Bennett had given him for Bella was all his own work. It was, thought Tom Lowry, a masterpiece of tact and sensitivity. Bennett spoke of his regret that he would not have the chance to get to know Bella better and wished that he had met her under different circumstances. Nowhere did he hint that he viewed her as no more than an innocent child, which would have been mortifying in the extreme for her. His sister might be a little sad that Will Bennett wasn't with Tom when he returned to Burfield, but she would treasure that letter as a token of perhaps the first man she had ever been sweet on.

It was cutting it fine, but Lowry managed to settle

everything and still be on the coach to Sherman that afternoon at four. It had been an entertaining excursion, but now it was time to return to real life.